Sex - The Unknown Quantity

Ali Nomad

Sex - The Unknown Quantity

1st Edition | ISBN: 978-3-75241-328-1

Place of Publication: Frankfurt am Main, Germany

Year of Publication: 2020

Outlook Verlag GmbH, Germany.

SEX = The Unknown Quantity

THE SPIRITUAL FUNCTION OF SEX

A New and Startling Interpretation of the Meaning, Scope and Function of Sex as Seen and Interpreted From the Inner or Cosmic Standpoint. A Work That Should Revolutionize the Thought of Today in its Relation to the Vital Mystery of Sex in All its Aspects. It Presents a Practical Solution to the Sex Problems of Everyday Life.

By

ALI NOMAD

1

PUBLISHER'S FOREWORD

To Our Readers:

We feel justified in claiming this work marks an epoch in the advanced thought of human evolution. Nothing has ever been written dealing with the problem of Sex which is at once so illuminating, convincing and satisfying. To our knowledge this particular view of the sex-subject has never before been presented, and, perhaps it could not have been, owing to the fact that it is only *now* in these days of higher thought, that such a view could be understood.

The author, Ali Nomad, is already well known to progressive readers as the writer of "Cosmic Consciousness," or, "The Man-God Whom We Await;" a work that has made its author famous by the reprint of its many editions.

There are signs of a new order in the relation of the Sexes already indicated upon the horizon of the World's consciousness as the result of the present world-conflict. *Today people are as ignorant of the subject of Sex as they are of God.* Both of these must be understood if the race is to progress beyond its present stage. Otherwise we shall pass into the long sleep of oblivion like all civilizations in the past leaving future generations to grapple with the same world problems.

True or *perfect* marriage is the most important attainment in the life of the individual.

The author demonstrates that perfect marriage is a scientific possibility and that legal marriage and divorce simply conform to civil laws. He very clearly outlines the reason why civilization makes little or no progress in dealing with the social evil and other sex problems.

The publishers place this book before an intelligent public, believing, that more *real* knowledge can be gained by its study, than by any other known method, because

First. The reader is brought face to face with himself, and nature.

Second. The reader can demonstrate the truth of the propositions set forth.

Third. The methods, rules, and laws have been verified by intelligent men and women who have lived the life.

Fourth. "Sex," The Divine Principle which all human beings should understand, has been presented in plain simple terms, and elucidated, so that the reader *cannot* fail to understand the true path of moral progress.

This volume is not a romance, a fairy tale nor a dream intended to entertain or amuse, but a scientific instruction which will elevate the individual and the race, develop self respect, self control, morality and love. If the propositions presented by the author are correct—let the standards be changed; *if* the propositions are *in*correct, they will not disturb the standards of today.

THE PUBLISHERS.

INTRODUCTION

No phase of civilization can rise to the highest possibilities as long as the average mental attitude toward the most vital, the most important and the most sacred function of our being, is one of shame, sinfulness, lust and uncleanness.

Even among those who are conscientiously trying to establish better social conditions, there is a deplorable lack of anything like the proper attitude toward the problems of Sex, albeit there are evidences that our social consciousness is alive to the seriousness of the sex problem.

Many of our advanced thinkers and scientists are giving their attention to the subject, but it is a theme which has been so long neglected, so hedged about by false standards of morality; so fettered by the system of tabu, that a rational discussion of Sex apart from materia medica, or religion, is difficult.

Moreover, the physiological side of the sex question robs it of all the delicacy, and the intimacy and the beauty and romance which should by right, surround the function of sex-mating and which does surround a union that is pure and perfect. In this innate desire to share with the one and only possible mate, the intimate secrets of love, there is nothing of shame or apology—sentiments which alas, actuate the so-called "modest" man or woman of today.

Sex matters should, indeed, be held too sacred, too intimate for public discussion, whereas the present-day attitude holds that Sex is too indecent to be spoken of. When the subject is forced upon public attention as it so frequently is through tragic occurrences, the opinions expressed are both petty and puerile. They evade the truth and so avoid the issue. They deal with effects only, are satisfied with offering suggestions as to ways and means of suppressing these effects, instead of going to the root of the matter and realizing that all the tragedies that spring out of Sex are due to wrong teaching and thinking in regard to the sex-function. That which we reverence, and hold sacred, we do not profane. Until Sex is established in its rightful place, as the holy and divine creative power of this universe, we will be shocked and horrified with sex-tragedies.

It is a pity that the physiological and hygienic aspect of Sex has to be discussed at all, but it is necessary that all sides of the subject must be presented to meet the great variety of minds, but it is our contention that if the spiritual quality of Sex were recognized and understood, there would be no need for any other view, because if Sex were recognized as the sacred, and holy and spiritual function *that it is*, disease and sinfulness would disappear as

4

the mist before the sun.

In the meantime the subject must be discussed from all points of view.

It must be permitted to thrive in the light and thus it will flower into the perfection of the spiritual seed that generated it.

In the meantime, the debasement of all things connected with sex must be aired, discussed, and weeded out, until a sane and normal and reverential recognition of the universality and the eternality of Sex, is engendered in the minds of men and women and growing youths and transmitted to the children yet unborn.

"Sex contains all," says Walt Whitman. "Bodies, souls, meanings, proofs, purities, delicacies, results, promulgations, songs, commands, health, pride, the maternal mystery, the seminal milk; all hopes, benefactions, bestowals; all the passions, loves, beauties, delights of earth; all the governments, judges, gods, followed persons of the earth; these are contained in sex as parts of itself and justification of itself.

"Without shame the man I like knows and avows the deliciousness of his sex; without shame the woman I like knows and avows hers."

Many well-meaning persons see in the words of the "good grey poet," only an immodest and brazen shamelessness. But these are mental perverts and are to be pitied; they see "through a glass darkly" and everything looks black with decay; they are trying to build an eternal future upon a foundation of tissue paper; they are seeking to encompass immortal life by denying the very beginning and source of all life—Sex; they are attempting the impossible feat of foisting upon the world an ideal of Heaven from which they have extracted the very essence of Heaven itself, although nothing on earth or from divine sources justifies such an idea.

Possibly our civilization has proceeded on the plan of leaving until the last the most important thing in an ideal community and it may be that we shall do the necessary reform work in this department all the more thoroughly for having so long neglected it.

In the following chapters the physiological and hygienic side of the subject has been avoided as there is much sound advice already issued pertaining to this phase of the sex question, and it is our contention that the world must be brought to recognize the spiritual, and sacred function of Sex, as the basis of reformation or regeneration, before the Kingdom of Love shall be established upon the earth as it is in celestial spaces.

THE AUTHOR.

CHAPTER I

SEX UNIVERSAL AND ETERNAL

The fundamental basis of the universe is Sex.

Sex is the fulcrum upon which our life-activities turn. It is the life of Man and of planets, and ignorance of the laws of Sex is the cause of death of both. It is the conjunction of the forces of attraction and repulsion; the positive and negative; the centripetal and centrifugal forces which hold stars and planets in their orbits—or rather, it is the two expressions of the one power, which is both male and female, the eternal bi-une sex principle which is *Life*.

The law of attraction everywhere, from that of the sun and the earth, to that of the iron and the magnet, the "affinity" of the various gases and liquids, is founded upon Sex. Cohesion is but another name for copulation, and repulsion is absence of the power of contact. The law of attraction and cohesion everywhere is the law of sex-activity. "The law of conjugality is the basis of every force in nature," says a scientist. Sex constitutes the eternal energy from which issue all the forms and differentiations which we see manifested in the visible universe, and it is equally the foundation of the realms invisible.

Sex is the algebracial X—the unknown quantity which defies analysis.

Plato is said to have observed that "the son of man is written all over the visible world in the form of an X;" and also that "the second coming of Christ is rightly symbolized by a cross." The cross is but another form of the X—the eternal bi-une sex-principle in action.

The Female Principle attracts to a central union; draws toward and within itself. The home is established and maintained by the female element; the nest is the special property of the female bird. Thus the Female Principle best expresses the highest love because the object of love is *union*. Hate scatters, disintegrates, destroys. Wherever the struggle between love and hate is seen, there we will find a lack of union. There may be marriage, but there will not be mating. True union must come from the Center of Life—from the spiritual Reality, which the physical only imperfectly shadows forth.

Involution is best described as feminine, and wherever we note the upward trend of the feminine element in Society, we may know that the earth is on its involutionary path; the end of a cycle is at hand, and social unrest and marital upheaval are inevitable, because Love is in the ascendant and love demands *union*—not merely matrimony.

The Ancients sought to express the never-beginning and never-ending law of Sex by the symbol of the serpent with its tail in its mouth, forming a circle. The resemblance of the male sperm to the spiral convolutions of the serpent in motion, doubtless gave rise to the adoption of the serpent as a symbol of sex-worship. The retention and transmutation of the sex-force is typified by the serpent forming a circle. The circle represents the attainment of godhood—victory over death through *regeneration.*

It has been said that the most primal instinct is that of hunger, but without Sex there would not be even the urge toward physical sustenance. Sex is therefore both the urge and the answer to all instincts.

There is a very general idea that Sex is a physical function only. It is almost universally taught that when the life of the body ceases, sex-life ceases with it. Even among metaphysicians, who believe in the continuity of life after death, the absurd doctrine is taught that Sex has no place or part in spiritual life, that "there is no marriage nor giving in marriage" after death.

This idea has been a powerful deterrent in keeping the race from seeking the higher areas of spiritual consciousness. Lack of mere physical vitality has erroneously been estimated as evidence of spirituality. Chastity has unfortunately been counterfeited by mere physical restraint, resulting in a type of human being whom the healthy, normal person instinctively refuses to emulate, deferring as long as possible the attainment of that which has been presented to the mind as "spirituality."

Let it be understood at the outset of this presentation of the problem of Sex that we state emphatically, that Sex is an eternal verity. Its spiritual function is not *less* but infinitely *more* than that which we glimpse on the physical plane of life-expression.

Far from outgrowing what we know as human love, we add thereunto a million fold, refining, purifying and *intensifying* the sex instinct until it bears a relationship to the average instance of sex-expression, analogous to that which the single-celled organism bears to intellectual man. If we will keep in mind the fact that Life in all its degrees of manifestation is like the ascending notes of the musical scale, we will be able to get a more comprehensive idea of the spiritual function of the sex-urge. We will realize that we can not mark a too distinctive separation between the various phases of life-manifestation.

We imagine that the physical life is widely at variance with the mental, the psychical, or the spiritual, when as a matter of fact each blends into the other, when we rightly understand their place and purpose, as harmoniously as the notes of the musical scale blend into the grand compositions of the Masters.

"As above so below, and as below so above," is a truism which we may safely take as our first maxim. Whatever we note as a fundamental principle of this external life which we cognize with our five senses (senses which merge so into the psychical that we know not always where the line demarks) has a permanent place in the Cosmos. Therefore we must conclude that a fact so universal as that of sex, and sex-attraction, must be grounded in something more stable, more permanent and enduring than the mere creation of physical forms.

Protoplasm, the only living substance, is found everywhere in the visible world and its universality is symbolical of the invisible worlds as well. Transparent, colorless, it contains within itself the mystery of reproduction. It forms the basis of the vegetable and the animal kingdoms. It is seen in bone and muscle and fibrous tissue, and protoplasm may be said to contain within its cells the principles of both sexes. It is not sexless, but bi-sexual; not neuter but masculine-feminine. Every form of life has sex, and in some rare instances both sexes are present in one form. This does not mean that there is another phase of sex unclassified, but rather it proves the union in one *Whole Entity* of the two distinct principles, and by this fact of the "twain made one" we may know that Sex is the very crux of the cosmic law; that not only does it survive the mere physical expression of the law, but that the object of the sex-function is the spiritual union of the two principles, a male and a female entity, forming one complete and perfect Being—the true representative of the bi-une Being whom we know as God.

Absolute and perfect union is possible only at the center, the crux, of Being. This truth is represented by the algebraical X, the symbol of spiritual sex-union. Therefore sex relationships which do not have for their crux spiritual as well as temperamental affinity, are not final, or eternal, however beautiful they may be; and there are many sex-relationships which are pure and sacred even though they do not fulfil this highest of all relationships, that of spiritual counterparts.

Let us consider for a moment the universality of Sex as we see it expressed in all the variety of forms and throughout all the species, and in so doing we may trace the ever upward trend of the law of sex-attraction, and discover, if we have the eyes to see, the evident plan and purpose of the cosmic law as it tends toward completement and perfection in the type of the man-god whom the world has long looked for and who we believe is here.

If we look at the expression of Sex from the viewpoint of the physical only, instead of basing our observations from the interior, the spiritual, outward to the physical, we might conclude that the function of sex was designed for no other purpose than that of procreation, since care of the young increases with the upward trend of life-manifestation.

Beginning at the lower forms of life, such for example as the fish, we find as a general thing an indifference to the fate of the eggs deposited by the female, which is in keeping with the prolific and almost unconscious generation of these tiny evidences of the law of Sex. A fish laying more than a million eggs in a season is naturally rather careless about what becomes of them. Apparently no higher sentiment actuates this form of life than an unconscious and merely instinctive urge to perpetuate the species—the lowest expression of Love—and yet the germ of Love, the Creator and Preserver is there, and a well-defined law of attraction and repulsion is evident from the fact that as an almost general thing the male will not fertilize eggs other than those of his own species. But even in these low forms, we see the evidence of that higher expression of Love which presages the god-like quality of self-sacrifice. Some species of fish, notably the stickle-back and the bass, make nests and mother their young.

In those forms of life which are supposed to be insensate, we find the universal law of sex-attraction and repulsion. The pollen from an oak tree, for example, may be blown about by the wind and may light upon a plant which is far removed in species from its own; but if such be the case, no fertilization takes place. The fundamental law of Love is to attract to itself *its own*; that which belongs to it by right of Cosmic law and order and justice.

All the inharmony of our social life comes from the attempt to appropriate and *possess* that which, in the final analysis, in the Absolute, is not ours. When the majority of Mankind shall have mastered this lesson, the human race will enter upon its true spiritual life. The psychic mind with which man alone of all earth's creatures is supposed to be endowed will have conquered the instinctive mind, and the higher expression of love which would protect and preserve, and *leave free*, will have gained supremacy over selfishness and the desire for possession.

In bird-life we find this higher type of love almost universal. Parental love, that exquisite and refined flower from the seed of sex-attraction, characterizes the bird and we may readily agree that Paradise would be incomplete without birds and flowers as well as babies.

Considering the birds as an infinitely finer type of sex-expression than that offered by any other of the forms of life below man, we note with satisfaction the all-important point, namely, that the sex-urge is more diffused and lasting, and of a finer quality than that of the mammals.

The bird woos its mate with the beauty of its plumage and the harmonious notes of its love-call. Its desire finds so many esthetic ways of expressing itself; in tender pleadings; in cooing promises; in continuous evidences of care and protection. Nor does its intense love, vital as it is, exhaust itself in concentrated expression, but it softens and ripens into something that so closely resembles our ideals of spiritual love, that we are not surprised to find the emblem of the dove employed throughout the history of the world, as the spiritual symbol of pure and holy love. Well, indeed, may human beings learn from the birds the lesson of the higher type of sex-mating, which finds fruition in their mutual love for and care of their progeny. Nor does the love-life of birds cease with sex-expression. It permeates all their intercourse.

The trait which distinguishes the spiritual man from the animal man is analogous to that of the birds; namely, that of finding a deep and lasting joy in the presence of the loved one; in sympathizing with each other's ideals; listening with devoted attention to each other's words; contacting, as it were, each other's *inner nature*, rather than obeying the merely animal urge of procreation. And above all, in the common aim of altruistic thoughtfulness for the little lives which their love has brought forth.

Thus nature serves the cosmic law, which aims to raise the sex-instinct from the incomplete and unsatisfying plane of physical contact, to that of spiritual union—a wide gulf seemingly; but who would not strive to bridge it, did he but realize what spiritual union with the Beloved One means?

CHAPTER II

SEX WORSHIP AND SEX DEGRADATION

Every form of religious worship, from pre-historic time down to and inclusive of the present century, and among all races, savage and civilized, has been founded upon Sex—the inevitable, the inviolable, the unescapable, and the unfathomable mystery of Creation.

Nor should this fact be distasteful to the most refined. An intelligent review of the many evidences that prove this truth will not shock the sensibilities of the most devout worshipper of an unknown and unseen God. What can be more beautiful and more holy, more worthy of our highest reverence and adoration, than the mystery of birth, whether that birth be the growth of a flower from a tiny seed planted in the womb of Mother Earth, or the birth of a tiny human life from the seed Love sows in the womb of the human mother? The only shocking thing about the matter is that there are persons who can be "shocked" at contemplation of this wonderful and beautiful mystery. It is shocking and deplorable that so many are still so far away from spiritual consciousness, that the beauty and the purity of the miracle of Sex is unrecognized by them.

With all due respect to the highest types of religious creeds which survive today, we are bound to concede that the very first form of worship which prevailed upon this earth was the purest as it was the simplest. Truth is simple. Deception introduces us into a maze of complexities. Nature worship prevailed we know not how many centuries previous to the dawn of historic records. All allegorical literature makes constant allusion to "The Golden Age," evidently referring to a time before that which has come down to us in sacred literature, as "The Fall of Man." The first conception of a supreme power, something higher and more perfect than Man himself, originated in the mystery of Sex; not only in the sex-function as exercised by Man, but also in the evidences of sex seen in plants and animals.

It became evident to the earliest races that the human being was after all only a progenitor. Somewhere there must be a First Cause. The vital spark which gave to the seed its power to bring forth was seen to be beyond and above the control of physical man, and the natural and inevitable inference was drawn that there was some power greater than that of human beings—a power manifesting itself in the act of procreation. At this early stage in Man's efforts to know God, the Female Principle was deified, because out of the womb of the woman issued the little life. Thus the symbol of the "virgin with the child" became the symbol of worship; the word "virgin" then having a somewhat different meaning from that which we give it today, although we may trace the analogy in our use of the term "virgin soil," signifying fecundity. The virgin and child then, popularly supposed by those whose prejudices prevail over their desire for Truth, to have originated with the birth of Jesus of Nazareth, antedates history, as an object of worship.

Let us here again emphasize the fact that the very persistence of this symbol as a pronounced part of our Twentieth Century traditions, and reverence, offers proof of the fact that whatever is true is also enduring. Truth is eternal and defies extinction. Love, although defiled and scorned, will lift Mankind out of Hell.

The symbol of the mother with the child the very earliest of all symbolic worship is also the truest and most consistent with the ideals of spiritualized Man when we realize its higher significance. At first, for the obvious reason that woman was the recipient and the nurse of the seed, woman was regarded as a higher type than man; she alone was supposed to possess the creative energy. This was ultimately reversed and Man was thought to be the sole custodian of the reproductive power.

Thus the age-long warfare between the sexes began—a warfare which, if it had any foundation in Reality, must have resulted long since in race-extinction. But despite this degrading warfare men and women have continued to attract each other in varying degrees of love, until now the future offers a golden promise of *union*. As long as primitive man kept to nature worship, deifying earth as the mother who brought forth the grains and fruits for her childrens' sustenance, religious practices were devoid of sacrifice and strife. The advent of springtime when the earth awakened from her long sleep and the period of gestation began when the seeds were planted, or when from Nature's own laws they were reproduced without the aid of man, was the occasion of thanksgiving and rejoicing with general merry-making and general good-will. Again, in harvest time there was feasting and rejoicing and music and dancing; and we have no reason to believe that this very natural method of showing their gratitude and their happiness was accompanied by any suggestion of sacrifice or propitiation.

There is the best of evidence to support the claim that all the early Deities were female and in all Mythology the earth is adored as the "Divine Mother." The earliest Venus, worshipped as the goddess of Universal Womanhood, was represented with a beard signifying her androgynous character.

Venus worshipped as "the soul of the world" was said to be the "parent of all things, the primary progeny of Time, the most exalted of all the Deities." Neith, Minerva, Athena, Ceres, Cybele, all worshipped as the first of all the Deities, were represented as female, and to this day we refer to the qualities of wisdom, light, truth, and virtue as feminine.

Even the sun is said to have been at one time worshipped as feminine, as were all deities; but later, when it was shown that the sun apparently fertilized the fecund earth, the gender was changed, and in succeeding ages, when the male principle had become dominant as a deific symbol, the earth was said to be but the nurse which cradled and cared for the generic power resident in the male. Thus woman from her lofty height of the one and only deity gradually sank to the level of the nurse maid, permitted to care for man's offspring.

While the Female Principle of Sex was worshipped as the "giver of life," the heads of families were female and descent was traced from the mother only. The male parent was scarcely more than an intruder and the necessity to please the entire family and, above all, the mother-in-law, the generic head of the family has left its mark upon the masculine mind, even unto this far-off day, when by virtue of this ordeal of primitive man, an idea seems to exist, that a mother-in-law is to be both feared and dreaded, if not propitiated. When we contemplate the persistence of those traits of human nature that have prevailed among all races and throughout all ages, we are easily persuaded that time is a delusion, and that Eternity is Now. As it was yesterday it is today and will be tomorrow in all that is really fundamental.

From the refined simplicity of nature worship there gradually evolved a phase of worship, which in the beginning had for its basic principle an exalted ideal of the purpose and the powers of the female sex-function; but this ideal sunk to the level of debauchery and sex-degradation, in which the symbol of the female sex-organ of generation was worshipped, literally, although not reverently; and yet from the fact that it is only upon the temples and in the groves dedicated to worship that are found the carvings of the generative organs of either and sometimes of both sexes, it is evident that the most exalted motives first actuated the worshippers.

The sex organs, representing the mystery of creative life, or the Deity, would naturally be held in reverence by nature-children, and it must be conceded that this attitude of mind toward the wonderful miracle of creative energy is worthy of our emulation. As we look back over the pages of history, we note the tendency of human nature to fall far short of ideals; we mistake the letter for the spirit; we get lost in the trap of the senses, and we miss the higher and more exalted planes of our ideals.

From yoni worship (worship of the female organ of generation), with all the privileges and perquisites which such honor bestowed upon woman, there came the inevitable revolt, which comes in course of time, from all tyranny and special privilege, whether it be individual, national, racial, sexual, or supernatural. Thus there was established a "new religion," and this time it was the male organ which was deified as the symbol of eternal life, of creative

13

energy. In many instances both symbols were represented, but for the most part the same subtle struggle for supremacy, the remnants of which we note today among the different religious creeds and sects, waged, and waxed stronger, with time and opposition. Which was the more worthy of deification —the yoni, or the phallus? Woman, or man?

The Ionians, seeking religious freedom from the persecutions of the phallic worshippers in India persisted in their adherence to yoni worship, and from them dates the Eleusirian mysteries, which were celebrated in Athens down to a comparatively late date. The Eleusirian festivals represented the survival of the purest ideals of nature worship, before the warfare between the yoni and the phallic worshippers had brought both ideals into degradation.

There is a point in this festival, which the Greeks called Thesmophoria and which is derived from the more ancient festival of Ceres (the goddess of Life and Law), which we are anxious to have noted here, because it marks a golden thread which runs throughout the entire fabric of the sex-problem. This point is the fact, that the rites and ceremonies of this festival were performed by "virgins distinguished for their purity of life." Very rarely were men admitted to the inner secrets of the Eleusirians.

Another important point is that this ceremony was performed in honor of the androgynous character of the goddess, as it was declared that the power to bring forth a child without the co-operation of the male belonged exclusively to the exalted or perfected woman, which is to say the goddess. Another translation and interpretation of this ceremony claims that it was prophecied in these festivals, that a time would come in the history of the world when a woman would so conceive and bring forth a child and that when that time should come the question as to which sex was supreme would be forever settled and that purity and peace would reign upon earth.

This part of the record may easily have been either an interpolation to sustain the claim of the miraculous birth of Jesus, or it may have been simply the defiant fling of the vanquished to the victor, because phallic worship was in the ascendant. It is, however, recorded, that not an instance can be cited in which the honor of initiation into the Eleusirian mysteries was conferred upon a bad man; nor of any man violating the secrets of the inner temples of the Eleusirians. This gives rise to the hope that the ideal of this spiritually exalted sect, in the midst of almost universal degeneracy, was not so much that of female supremacy, as of purity; that their ideal included the pure and perfect union of male and female—the only ideal that will, or can, redeem the world to a life of peace and love.

The festivals of Carthage were said to be similar to those of Eleusis. For a period of several days during the time set apart for the festivities, public feasts were prepared in honor of the deific nature of Man, which, it was pointed out, was his prerogative only by virtue of inward purity and strict adherence to high ideals of truth and honor.

Crowning all the religious observances of the Ancients, whether expressed in the legends of the sun-myths or of star and serpent worship, we find the universally recognized fact that only those qualities of mind and soul can be expected to endure, or reach immortal godhood, which are of an exalted character. Which is to say what the present day orthodox creed says, that immortality belongs only to those who are pure in heart.

From the Eleusirian festivals is derived our custom of taking holy communion, the symbol of the Lord's supper; albeit the substitution of the male principle in the Christian ceremony attests the fact that the phallic symbol ultimately supplanted the yoni, as a deific symbol. Phallic worship reached its height during Hebrew and Assyrian supremacy, and was perpetuated by Greek and Roman materialism. Superstition is nothing more than Truth degenerated by men from a spiritual to a material application. That which is held in awe and reverence by any race; that which is embodied in the traditions of every tribe on the globe; that which persists throughout all times will be found to have a fundamental basis of truth, no matter how obscured it may be by the ignorance with which it is so frequently associated.

The sacredness of Sex, as exemplifying the Supreme Creative Energy, underlies all the traditional ideals of man, from the fetishes of the Central African savage to the cathedral spires which rise above the din of our modern commercial civilization. The prejudiced and the superficial observer of so-called "heathen" rites and ceremonies records only the superstitions, and sees only the evidences of depravity and savagery. He overlooks the fact that the spirit of the idea conveyed may have been the highest ideal of an early race which has sunk, as have all races during certain periods of the world's evolution into the depths of a materialism, from which all races are today emerging.

All mystic truths are expressed in symbolism. It has been said that these truths are "veiled;" this is true only because the observer has not yet learned to speak the language. The universal language is symbolism. In the early Egyptian, the Indian, and the Hebrew religions, the fundamental idea was the two generating principles (or we might say the two aspects of the One principle) of generation. The two in spiritual *union* represented the Infinite— the Deity. The Hebrew word "Elohim" is plural, and means male and female united, forming the One Perfect and Complete Being. This union is the "Holy of Holies" of the ancient mystics and alchemists. We see its reflection and its persistence today in the Catholic service of the Mass, where the priest raises the Eucharist as the "Holy of Holies" in which is generated the Christ-man, and before whom all human devotees bow the head that they may not look upon the perfection and beauty of its pure radiance. Neither is the priest supposed to touch the chalice with uncovered hands. He prepares himself by fasting and prayer before he mounts the altar upon which this "Holy of Holies" is hidden from view.

The pattern of the Eucharist with its golden circle and radiations is easily recognizable by any one who is familiar with the symbols of yoni worship. Nor should this fact be distasteful to any one, although it is either concealed, or flatly denied by the Church, since it is only through the elevation of the sex-function that the Christ-man can be born into the physical realms. The reason that this truth is either concealed or denied by the Church is due to the influence of Greek and Roman civilization, which subjugated woman to the control of man. This debasement of woman reached its culmination under Roman rule and is unquestionably the psychic cause of the fall of the Greek and Roman empires.

If we will but take home to ourselves the important lesson that neither sex is fundamentally, or even relatively, superior, but only different; that no race is permanently in advance of another, but that each little group and class of humans has its particular contribution to the sum of knowledge, we will have done much toward freeing the mind from the shackles of ignorance—that darkness which obscures our inner vision. Let this truth penetrate the egotism of so-called civilized races. Let it sink into the minds of the men and women of this century: we are of service to the world in proportion as we are different and not identical. In the direct ratio of our individuality is our contribution to the work of the cosmic law, which is seeking to lift the planet earth out of its undeveloped state into celestial light.

The symbol of the Eucharist, occupying as it does an important place in a religious system which is otherwise essentially masculine, is one of the many evidences of the persistence of Truth. For approximately four thousand years, phallic worship has predominated over the earlier ideal, which was embodied in the "virgin of the spheres," the emblem of the Female Principle as eternal motherhood; and in the sacred character of androgynous plants and flowers, which were characterized as feminine, such, for example, as the lily, the lotus, and the fleur de lis. These flowers are still regarded as more or less sacred, and they are called feminine, although really androgynous.

The lotus, long held sacred because of its androgynous character, has been regarded as typical of the One Perfect One, because it is supposed that the lotus reproduces itself without the male pollen. But close examination of the flower will show that the little seed-vessel in the center of the flower is

16

shaped like a pine cone, in which are tiny cells too small to let out the seeds as occurs in most plant and seed life; these tiny seeds having no outlet, shoot when ripe into new plants, the bulb of the plant being the matrix or womb of the new life. Thus it is evident, that although the two sexes are not as pronounced in the lotus as in the lily, yet the bulb and the cone are both present in the lotus, making the plant bi-sexual, and not feminine alone.

Our modern Easter festival, in which the lily is recognized as the representative par excellence of the renewal of abundant life and energy, the "sacred" flower, is a tribute to the Feminine Principle in the Deity, as the lily like the lotus is called feminine, although in reality bi-sexual.

The lily and the Eucharist have survived the centuries in which the male principle has dominated, as the one true and only God—the giver of life, the energizing power of Creation—and the lily and the Eucharist are both representative of the Female principle.

Historians mark the beginning of the worship of the *One True God*, defined philosophically as the "Monistic" God-idea, from the building of the tower of Babel, and we may here note in passing that in the earliest references to this tower, there is no allusion to anything suggestive of "confusion of tongues." The name unquestionably came from "babil" meaning "the gate of God." Thus only is its meaning obvious, and consistent with the worship of the lingam and phallus which obtained at that time. It is also evident that the phallic worshippers borrowed the simile of "the gate of God" from the worshippers of the yoni, who based their claim to truth upon the indisputable fact, that out of the womb comes the life of plant, and animal, and man.

The architecture of, and the inscriptions on, the tower of Babel show conclusively that it was a monument to the victory of the phallic worshippers over the yoni, proving that the "one true and only God" was male. From that time also God has been alluded to as "He," although in the Oriental countries, and particularly among the Hindus, we find repeated allusions to the Deity as "The Divine Mother," and all the higher qualities are spoken of as feminine. It is because of this fact also, that we note the spread of Oriental religions and philosophies in this day of Woman's uprising. The Orientals retained the divinity of the female principle in theory, but not in fact.

Sex-worship is contemptuously alluded to in modern literature as "strange and erotic ideas," or words equally condemnatory. But this is an absurd stand, since nothing could be more natural than that the mystery of Creative Life should arouse our interest and our wonder; and it certainly ought to enlist our highest reverence. It becomes erotic only when men fail to worship in "spirit and in truth," and when the letter of the ideal survives, and the spirit is ignored. It becomes not only erotic but destructive when it involves a fight for supremacy between the male and the female. When the spirit of union shall prevail, which it must in a perfected world, no higher form of religious aspiration can be imagined than that in which the miracle of birth is reverenced and idealized. Then, and not until then, will the family be what it should be, and Love, the one and only true God, be worshipped.

The trinity in unity has been a widespread and persistent part of all religions, from which fact we may logically infer that this ideal has a permanent place in the sum of human knowledge. Truth is often obscured, but it can never be hidden from the eyes that are seeking the light. The rightful interpretation of those ancient and obscured truths, erroneously classified as "myths" and "superstitions," will reveal a universal truth, and will also show their relation to modern concepts.

But while we note a vague recognition of the female element in all our modern religious systems, the general acceptance of the God-idea as monistic and the gender of this monistic God as masculine betrays the domination of phallicism over yoni worship and also over that of the two principles in conjunction—the bi-une Deity. The tree is universally accepted as an emblem of life-energy. The upright shape of the tree; the sap which rises at certain periods from invisible sources; and the fact that the germinal power of the seeds of the fruits and trees is not destroyed by eating; all combined to make the tree symbolical of eternal life. The tree is either male or female, except in certain instances where it is, like the lotus, androgynous, such for example as the ash, which is the "sacred" tree of Scandinavia. Wherever a plant or a tree is found to be bi-sexual, it has been regarded as "sacred." The same idea is found throughout all myths, and all religious symbolism, namely: *the attainment of god-hood is reached when both sexes are united in one Being.*

The fuller meaning of this symbolical idea will be considered in a subsequent chapter; but for the present we are concerned with the history of sex-degradation from the pure ideal of nature worship to that of a monistic God whose gender is masculine. The pine tree, held sacred in many countries as a symbol of generation, and from which our own Christmas-tree is descended, is distinctively a male emblem, and its perennial green typifies the hope of Man that he too may manifest, in some form of life, the never-failing virility of the pine. The Latin name for the pine is pinus.

Thus from nature worship to phallic worship was but a step, but that step led to others. The pine, from the fact of its erect form; its spiral convolutions; its sap; its fruit; its renewal of activity; its root and veins; became a universally accepted emblem of the life-energy in man and in animals, and the gradual substitution of the male principle alone, for the androgynous idea as a symbol of Deity contributed to the idea of the inferiority of woman, until she finally became the slave and the plaything of man. The "virgin of the spheres," from her exalted mission as the Eternal Mother of the race, became at best but a secondary personality, and finally was refused any part in the symbol of the Holy Trinity.

Instead of father, mother and child, the Holy Trinity became "Father, Son and —Holy Ghost."

The early Romans must have been devoid of a sense of humor. But what of our modern Christian creeds, and their idea of the Holy Trinity composed of three male beings?

It is in Christian Science alone of all the modern creeds that the female principle is given a place co-equal with the male. Christian Science addresses the Deity as "Father-Mother-God," and their reverence for the woman who established the creed, as well as the Ionian type of architecture employed in their church edifices, are evidences of the re-establishment of the female principle in the God-idea. Christian Science is one of the most important instruments of the cosmic law in the present-day dethronement of the male principle as the only true God.

So permeated with this male God-idea is every branch of our modern thought; so enwrapped with the glamour of worship, that we hardly notice the one-sidedness of the ideal. Tradition is a powerful hypnotist.

Many members of the Masonic fraternity fail utterly to understand the symbolical language of their mosques and the phallic and yoni emblems which constitute their decorations. Notable among these emblems are the pomegranate; the lotus; the circle; the crescent; the swastika. The cone-shaped towers, that rise above the mosques, with their protruding heads, vein-tipped; the central symbol identical with the mound of Venus; denote the preservation of the Egyptian ideal, which venerated both sexes as co-equal. It is easy to realize why the Jews were driven out of Egypt when we remember that they refused to worship the Egyptian ideal of God as bi-sexual, but persisted in rearing the phallic symbol alone, denying the female principle a place in the God-head.

It is also significant that side by side with the present-day Feminist Movement we find the revival of Egyptian fashions; Egyptian architecture; Egyptian philosophies and religions. Even Cubist art, which in itself could make no possible appeal to recognition on its artistic merits, has been received with much publicity, if not with acclaim. Cubist art is a lineal descendant of Egyptian art, and so closely resembles its far-off ancestry as to seem to have bridged the centuries and connected us as if by telephone with the days of ancient civilization. Our drama and our popular songs have responded to the

Egyptian thought-wave. Talismanic jewelry, so essentially Egyptian, is in vogue, and on every sign board advertising breakfast foods, tobacco and what not (so essentially an American custom) we find the modernized use of Egyptian symbols, notably the swastika.

The swastika, the earliest form of the cross, found in every country and in every out-of-the-way corner of the globe, is fundamentally, originally and pre-eminently a bi-une sex symbol, and although volumes have in recent years been written on its history and meaning, the whole story may be summed up by examining its form and by realizing its antiquity and its universality.

The two sex principles, joined in the center of the four arms or legs, of the cross, accomplish that which is said (and truthfully if taken on the physical plane only) to be impossible of accomplishment—they square the circle. A circle is emblematical of completeness. Aum, the Absolute, the Omniscient, is always typified by a circle. To "square the circle" means esoterically to have reached godhood, and this can be accomplished only by the male and female *united* in spirit. The swastika is essentially a bi-une sex symbol although it has been sometimes called male and sometimes female, according to its shape, which varies with the various meanings ascribed to it. Primitive man was not prolific in language, and one symbol expressed many ideas according to its varied form and position.

The original form of oath was to swear by the sacred power of the generative organs, and we may readily conclude that this power was conceded to be vested in the male only, from the fact that we still "testify" when under oath and although the Bible has been substituted for the generative organs, as an outward expression of our recognition of the Creative Principle, we note that the Bible is made up of "testaments," which stand for its "sacredness."

Evidently it was only after the advent of the male God that oaths and vows and pledges were necessary. Previous to that time, a man's word was reliable. It was inevitable that an ideal of the Supreme Creative power of the universe so one-sided, and so lacking in the essential of union, must degenerate into mere licentiousness and animalism; and it is estimated that about six hundred years B.C. the level of debauchery and vileness reigned. So-called religious rites and ceremonies were nothing more than orgies of sex-degradation.

The ideal of godhood as nothing higher than masculine virility and power evidenced by the number of his progeny, naturally reduced woman to the lowest depths of slavery, since she was nothing more than a receptacle for man's seed. Of course one wife was insufficient and a man's claim to divinity was best expressed by profligacy—an ideal which is rife even today among those, whose consciousness is bounded by nothing higher than the conception of the animal nature of man.

20

Whence came this wonderful thing manifested as generative power? What did it feed upon? These were natural queries. In seeking the answer the idea originated that in the blood was to be found the secret of the generative fluid. This idea arose from the evidence that as old age conquered man's physical strength, his blood became weakened and the supply insufficient.

This was accompanied by a loss of generative activity, and thus, they argued, the power that made man god-like (the creative energy) left him. This was indeed a calamity greater than we in this generation realize, although we know that old age with consequent cessation of physical vigor is the dread enemy of the undeveloped man. Even our supposedly advanced thinkers have the absurd idea that sexual-energy dies with the physical body. The few who have risen to the place where they realize the truths made plain by soul-consciousness, know that old age is but physical; that it is the vacation time between the functions of physical activity and that of the soul-life. Old age is the wise provision of the Cosmic Law which compels those who will not do so of their own volition and wisdom, to transmute the life-energy into higher channels. If the race knew enough to consciously transmute the creative sex-energy into an interior function, there would come to pass the time prophecied by St. Paul when Man shall consciously "lay down his body and take it up again."

There are spiritually advanced men and women today who can consciously leave the physical body as they do the house in which they live, while they visit distant places, annihilating space. To these the body is no more than a garment. Thus death is overcome and the knowledge attained that we are souls using a physical body; that death does not in itself confer upon any one either immortality or youth or love, but that these may be acquired by acts of virtue and unselfish service—not as payment or reward for unwilling work, but as the result of unfailing law, which gives what we demand.

What we demand we naturally work for. If we serve Love, we get the coin in which Love pays as naturally as we get the checks signed by Jones when we work for Jones, and by Smith when we work for Smith.

Death merely discloses our interior nature. If we have failed to transmute the life-energy into a love that is deeper than mere animal instinct; if we have missed the beautiful and the pure and the lofty idealism of Love, we will find ourselves as age-worn after death as before the change. But again we may note a wise provision of the Cosmic Law, for it is almost impossible for a human being to live through many years of life without having loved some person or some thing with at least a spark of unselfish love. Fortunately almost every one is better interiorly than he appears to our limited vision. The most depraved of mortals has his moments of the higher vision.

From this deduction of inquiring primitive man, namely that the blood was the source of procreative virility, it is easy to trace the logical result in the terrible practise of blood-sacrifice which reigned so long and which, carried from one nation to another, and engrafted into the God-idea, has come down to us in the story of the "sacrificial lamb," at length personified in Jesus, the Son of God, as a final act of propitiation.

The blood-atonement idea is naturally repulsive to civilized beings, and were it not that nearly every one who adheres to the old form of orthodox Christianity swallows theologic interpretation of the Bible as he would swallow a dose of castor-oil, by closing his eyes and holding his nose, the teaching as thus interpreted would be stopped by police authority. And yet we may readily trace the gradual descent of the God-idea of the ancients until it reached the culmination in the idea of sacrifice of a son of God Himself.

In their blind but eager groping for some means of escape from death, even as we of this day and generation are groping, the early races observed that birth was accompanied by blood; that as age came on and the blood became thin, and in the case of the female ceased to flow at certain reproductive periods, the power of generation ceased. What more natural to primitive man than that he should conceive the idea of sending back to this unknown and invisible power behind the veil of the sky the blood, which he must need to supply his creative energies? And when the sacrifice of animals was not sufficient for this God, they concluded that it must be because he required the blood of man.

And so at first the old and the sick and the deformed were sacrificed; but as it was seen that this did not answer the need, they began to sacrifice the young, and naturally the slaves were substituted for the aged, as affording more blood; and when this failed the idea came, that the sacrifice must be that of one who was innocent of the world, and so they selected a girl or a young man, who had been secluded and trained to the thought of sacrifice, and in whom the sex-function had been rigorously suppressed.

And still the old grew bloodless and death claimed his toll, and so they conceived the idea of voluntary blood-sacrifice, and we read of repeated occasions in which fanatical ones offered themselves freely on the sacrificial altars as atonement for the sins of their people. At length this contagion of sacrifice consummated in the idea that the only Son of God Himself became a voluntary offering to pay the final debt of transgression and set men free from death, that they might have eternal life, which to them meant life in the physical body.

It is not at all possible that Jesus had any such idea of his mission. He was far too illumined for that, even judging from the meager accounts which we have of his life and message. But when the story of his mission on earth came to be told and retold the idea of blood-sacrifice as *payment* for the privilege of physical virility, so implanted in the race-thought from centuries of such belief, could not die immediately, and thus it reaches us today adown the centuries and is re-told (though we trust not believed) in most of the Christian churches in this civilized century.

And yet there is an esoteric truth underlying this universal idea of sacrifice, and when we come to this in a subsequent chapter, we will better understand how and why it has persisted throughout the centuries.

CHAPTER III
PRESENT-DAY CONDITIONS: THE COSMIC CAUSE

From the study of ancient sex-worship to our twentieth century systems of religion; our scientific discoveries; our intellectual standards of philosophy and social ethics; and above all, perhaps, our marvelous commercial order, connecting, as it does, the entire globe, seems a far cry; but it is only another link in a chain and fits into the past as accurately and as inevitably as the morning follows the night.

There is an erroneous idea current that public institutions, such as law-courts, religious creeds, educational systems, reform movements, et cetera, are causes of race-advancement. As a matter of fact they are not causes but results. They do not determine progress; they reflect it.

Causes start from the Center and radiate outward. We may realize this more readily if we will remember that if we throw a pebble into a pool of water, it starts innumerable little waves which traveling outward, reach a point some distance from the central source, and if we were to see the outermost wavelet only, we might imagine that the disturbance begins and ends far from the place where the pebble was thrown.

This illustration explains the difference between the materialistic and the metaphysical points of view. The former notes the result, and the latter the cause of existing conditions. The mystical viewpoint takes into account the fact that there is a cosmic law which acts like a tidal-wave. Materialists call the action of this law "Evolution," assuming that its impetus comes from our physical activities. It is, in fact, from the Center or spiritual source of life that all power, all evolution, emanates. The spiritual is the intensity of power; the physical is the attenuated.

The term, "spiritual realms" suggests to the average mind a vaporous space where nothing happens; yet it requires only a little intelligent reflection to establish the fact that, as Paracelsus said long ago, "The mind is the workshop in which all visible life is formed." Our mental operations are silently, invisibly, carried on, and yet we see the effect of these silent plans and ideas in our noisy methods of locomotion; our architecture; our commerce—in all the avenues of our active civilization.

We wish to emphasize the point that every so-called advancement; every discovery; every improvement in moral ideals as well as in mechanics, and in those things that add to our physical comfort, comes from the center of Life.

The external but *reflects* the action of the Cosmic Law which uncovers the vast areas of consciousness and frees the human soul from the hypnotisms, and the limitations of the animal-mind.

Animal force is still strong in the world to-day, but it is not as strong as it appears to be, because much of the seeming indifference and cold-heartedness of the people, taken en masse, is due to the hurried, feverish and insistent demands of our external life.

Underneath the surface, in the realm of the sub-conscious activities, there is developing the spirit of unity; of sympathy; and a consciousness of our innate relationship. This realization comes to the surface in times of great stress and peril.

The whole trend of modern life symbolizes or reflects the *ideal* of unity, albeit the tooth and claw and growl of the animal in Man may be seen and felt and heard in the vain effort to postpone the inevitable dethronement of the animal force, which would dominate the weaker and appropriate for the personal self, the creation of brain and hand, much as the house-dog, satiated with over-feeding, buries the bone he cannot eat lest some hungry brother-dog shall get it. Nevertheless, despite the animal greed that still shows in our modern life, there is plenty of evidence that we are on the upward spiral that leads to unity —the effect of love.

The superficial observer, dominated by that instinct of fear which seems to be so ingrained in our animal nature that we are all slaves to it in some form or degree, sees in the present-day conditions a menace to what he believes to be the moral life of the race, and particularly as these conditions apply to the modern woman.

He sees women coming out of the seclusion of their "rightful sphere" and meeting men on terms of equality. He sees what he terms "immodest dress;" defiance of traditional ideas of etiquette and conduct; he notes what appears to be a disregard for the faith of our fathers; and, above all, a distaste for that special function of woman—child-bearing. The superficial observer, both male and female, feels great alarm.

But let us not be dismayed. Present day conditions, particularly as they relate to the female principle of Creation, but reflect the inevitable reaction from a one-sided course. The pendulum swings back again and ultimately we will strike a balance; from domination to unity; from struggle to harmony. Even American commercial life admits the value of a vacation time.

Present day conditions, then, are not chaotic or lacking in a well-defined purpose, even though they are unsettled. Anything that disturbs the seeming placidity of the surface always strikes alarm to the undeveloped mind.

Particularly in those phases of our modern life which directly affect women, or in which we may say, the Female Principle is especially concerned, we note a determined and united demand for freedom.

Woman's demand for political equality is but a shadowgraph as it were of the real demand which is the demand of the Divine Feminine throughout all manifested life, for recognition of equality, in the plan of creation. It is a symbol of the ideal of unity which finds expression in the commercial world in trusts and labor unions; in the "let us get together" plea of the various advocates of reform; of all those enterprises which are seen to most directly affect the entire human family.

That there are women who are blind to this fundamental idea of their demand for political equality is true; and it is also true that there are perhaps as many men as there are women who recognize the need of woman's political and social equality, but this only proves the fact which we have already emphasized, namely that it is not women as personalities, but the Female Principle throughout the universe that is at the root of the modern Feminist Movement. The male principle is not confined to the form of man, neither is the female principle always expressed in the form of woman. Many men exemplify more of the maternal instinct than do certain women; neither must it be assumed that this type of man is effeminate; or that the woman of Amazonian physique is more masculine in thought and habit than is the little frou-frou specimen of womankind who looks appealingly into the eyes of her male escort, beseeching protection from the rude stares which she has premeditatedly invited. Qualities are sexless and universal. It is only in their specific combinations that they adequately represent the masculine or the feminine gender.

Blessed are they who have learned the art of discrimination.

Broadly speaking, women are behaving in a manner which upsets all precedent and promises ultimate emancipation from restraint.

But is it not possible that women no longer need restraint if they ever needed it? Is it not possible that the world has grown up, and that both men and women may safely be allowed the freedom of self-government, with all possible mutual aid in the work of establishing an upright, free, and trustworthy science of right living?

That which is always in the future is never ours and if we are ever going to be free and happy and well-conditioned there is no reason why we should not make it soon.

Woman's demand for political equality is sometimes used as an excuse to lessen her dignity and her place in society. People who do this are of the same

26

type as those before whom Sex cannot be discussed intelligently because they do not realize the sacredness of Sex. They are a remnant of the ages which have passed and which have left their mark, in the idea of a half-sexed God, the "He," the spouseless Father who brought forth the visible universe apparently without co-operation with the Female Principle. This type of person prates much about the dangers of race-suicide, meaning thereby the increasing tendency to childlessness and not as should be taken into account the death rate among children who are born of diseased and unfit parents and brought into existence without the necessary conditions of sanitation, food and care.

Our national Eugenic societies are hampered by false ideas of what constitutes morality, being bound to uphold the tradition that the child that is born of married parents, no matter how diseased in body and deficient in mind, is better-born than is the offspring of unmarried parents, even though the latter may be a model of physical health and mental efficiency. Eugenics will remain limited in scope until such time as the entire world adopts "in spirit and in truth" the recent action of the European governments, and recognizes the legitimacy of all children however born.

And although the action of the European governments was born of nothing more humane than a war expediency in order that more soldiers might be bred, yet the effect of such a course will benefit the human race. It has at least set a precedent, and will in time be extended to all children born out of wedlock and will wipe out forever the cruel and unjust stigma that has attached to the child of unmarried parents. Thus it will be seen that even war has its good results, and although it seems a terrible price to pay for even so badly a needed reform as this, Humanity has always paid dearly for its willful blindness. It certainly should be evident to any sane mind that every child that is born into this world has a moral and a legal right to be here. Whatever may be said for or against parents, it is wicked stupidity to brand an innocent child with the epithet "illegitimate." The lowest animal has a right to be born. Many a beautiful and innocent child is denied that right.

If it has taken one of the most bloody wars in history to establish the right of birth, even so the struggle will not have been in vain, because this right, once established in the hearts of all Humanity, will forever do away with warfare. No doubt this assertion will sound far-fetched to many, but the future will see the vindication of this belief.

Birth is actually the most important function in life. If it is immoral to be born, no matter what the conditions of such birth, what possible chance have we to live morally? We cannot discriminate in dealing with the great fundamentals of life.

This truism, applies to all cosmic action. Nature's laws are inviolable. Nature says that the child of the king and the child of the beggar shall be born in the self-same way. The child of the unmarried mother and the child of the married mother come into the world in accordance with the self-same law of reproduction. Nature may not be always polite, but she is always truthful.

As long as there is any question of the "legitimacy" of any birth, Humanity as a whole cannot be otherwise than inferior, because Humanity cannot rise higher than the ideal of the average. Moreover we are so interdependent that the whole must be affected by the conditions of a part.

Birth is right, or it is wrong. It cannot be right under some circumstances and wrong under others. The primal laws do not take into account our ideas of respectability.

The question then arises: "Are we to consider it moral and legitimate for women to have children before they have been married?"

The obvious answer to this question is, that the mother must be permitted to decide this for herself, since no one has a right to do it for her. Our right of interference in so intimate a matter must begin only at the point where her conduct injures us. If an unmarried woman chooses to give birth to a child, neither you nor I, nor Society is injured, not even if the child becomes a charge of the state, because the cost of maintaining a child is far less than that of maintaining insane asylums and penitentiaries—both of which result from our mistaken attitude toward the sex-relation.

If we are permitted to answer the question of morality and legitimacy by generalities, we will say that any child that comes into the world *desired by the mother* is born in accordance with the highest possible concept of the moral law. Whenever Society, Church and Governments shall unite to wipe out the stain upon mother and child because of failure to comply with our marriage laws, a better race of men and women will people the earth, because the race-thought will be one of welcome with all that word implies; whereas at the present time, under our undeveloped ideas of morality, doubt, suspicion, and condemnation prevail, with all that these words imply.

When all mothers are honored all women will be willing to be mothers.

As long as dishonor attaches to any instance of motherhood, it is inevitable that motherhood will be avoided, even to the point of child-murder. Not that this practice is confined to the women who would be dishonored by becoming mothers. It obtains rather more perhaps among those women whose wealth and ease would seem to make motherhood desirable. Judging from surface conditions only, one might not see the connection. But that is the trouble with our modern life. We do not look deeply enough to deal intelligently with causes. We are always seeking to check effects.

The average human being is little more than a phonographic record of the dominant race-thought, and race-thought ideas are contagious.

Let us honor and provide for all mothers and all children and we will find that the birthrate will increase among the "rich and respectable," where now we note a determined desire to shirk the responsibilities of parenthood.

We need not fear that the number of unmarried mothers will be alarming. The first aid to true morality is honesty. Monogamy is the ideal relationship between men and women. But enforced relationships are neither ideal nor true. Ideal conditions can be established only between free human beings. Compulsion is death. Selection and choice mean life and health.

The man or the woman who is free, and particularly free from self-condemnation, is instinctively monogamous. Life in all its phases tends upward toward conscious and specific selection. Conscious selection must include love, and we may safely trust love. Love is inseparable from truth and fidelity. Without love, all the efforts of all the Eugenic Societies on earth will accomplish little, however well-meant their efforts. Eugenists confine their work to the physical aspect of the subject and as a matter of expediency deal with the effects of marriage and race-propagation in their relation to disease and degeneracy, ignoring the esoteric phase of the subject. Thus no real good can come of the Eugenic movement per se. Its contribution to Progress consists in its value as an "announcer" of a higher *ideal*, rather than a higher *order*. The higher order can come only by getting back to primal laws.

The fact should not be overlooked that the ancient Greeks were competent Eugenists. They effected wonderful results, too, in two important points of the well-balanced individual. They worked for beauty and intellect, both desirable adjuncts to a perfect race, but both also as cold as the marble statues which Greece gave to the world. Greek and Roman civilization toppled and fell because it was a civilization without foundation; it was built from the outside; it was like an old ruined house encased in a thin wall of beautiful marble, and set upon a high hill. It deceives the eye from a distance, but freezes the blood and congeals the soul when intimately known.

Greek and Roman civilization, based upon physical Eugenics, was unbalanced and could not endure, because it was a civilization of force; of dominance rather than of unity. There was no ideal of sex-equality, and therefore Love was regarded as the least important requisite in Eugenic marriage. It should be obvious that without the element of love, as the basis of selection, human reproduction must take on the same status as stock-breeding, which may for a time give the finest physical specimens of animal life, but which, if persisted in, finally results in decadence.

We have an example of the tendency to decadence from in-breeding of those types of humans which have the best advantages at least of education and refinement, whether or not those advantages are embraced. We refer to Royalty. We need only mention the illustrious example of Cleopatra to prove this. Cleopatra was the offspring of a marriage between a brother and sister— a custom which prevailed among ancient rulers to insure none but royal blood. Cleopatra we may well believe was both beautiful and intellectual, but it is also certain that she was abnormally lacking in conscience, in tenderness, in love. Her passions were those of the animal, and not of the soul.

In modern life, Spain and Austria both furnish discouraging data to exponents of "select" breeding. In fact it is thoroughly established that degeneracy is not the result of imperfect physical conditions only. The greatest villians are not infrequently both handsome and intellectual.

Bulwer Lytton well illustrates this fact in his character of "Margrave" in "A Strange Story." Margrave was a perfect and beautiful physical specimen. He possessed rare intelligence, but he had no soul and was utterly incapable of the finer sensibilities, which we instinctively classify as spiritual attributes.

Returning to a consideration of what has been termed the "unusual behavior" of the feminine half of mankind, we find that the chief end and aim of many women centers upon the problem of how to avoid maternity, quite upsetting traditional ideas regarding woman's rightful sphere, which began and ended in rearing a large family.

Women in all walks of life, rich and poor, wise and frivolous, selfish and unselfish—are refusing to bear children. The superficial observer rails against this, because he sees only the effect. He sees women living in fashionable hotels, if they are rich enough to afford it; if they are poor they establish a cheap imitation of this phase of semi-communal life in what is paradoxically known as "light" housekeeping, usually represented by one small dark room where the nearest delicatessen serves as a convenience, the public laundry minimizes domestic labor, and the department store supplies ready made, the family clothing, from undergarments to top coats. Under these conditions, whether of fashionable hotel suites or dark "light housekeeping," it is plain that children are not welcome.

Even those of the class found between these extremes are discouraged from rearing children, since city life tends more and more to apartments as a substitute for the home; and no well regulated apartment house is open to children. The average observer, as we say, notes these conditions, but fails to realize that there must be a cosmic cause for a condition so wide-spread.

There must be "something back of it," as we say of many things which we note in our every day life. Looked at from the surface only, these conditions seem deplorable and ultimately race-suicidal. But the cosmic law is always upward in tendency. We may safely trust it, if we will.

This does not mean that the conscious motive which actuates the average woman, who is able physically and financially to bear children and yet will not, is a high and noble one. The law deals with the planet, not directly with the individual; it acts upon the developed and the undeveloped with equal impartiality, even as the rain falls upon the just and the unjust alike.

Spiritually conscious persons realize the necessity for a change in human ethics. The world is in need of a more exalted ideal; an ideal in which equality shall be more nearly represented and they give themselves consciously to the task of assisting in this regenerating work.

The difference is not in the law itself, but in our comprehension of it. The curriculum of the school of life is unchanged. We graduate from it or we return for another term, according as we have mastered the studies. Applying this truth to the conditions just stated, and we see that this rebellion on the part of woman against child birth has two aspects. One is from apparent selfishness and lack of the temperamental quality, which has erroneously been attributed to women as an exclusive possession, namely, the maternal instinct.

The other aspect of woman's disinclination to maternity is due to a restless, vague but nevertheless determined desire on the part of the Feminine Principle, to wait until conditions are more equal. Sometimes we find women, who are perfectly awake and consciously aware of the cause of their "brazen sterility," as a virile writer has caustically termed it; but more often the conscious mental attitude is lacking and they merely obey blindly the dominant race-mind.

Women know much more in the depths of their souls than they can put into words. A part of this knowledge is the fact that child-bearing is not a function limited to the physical, the mortal plane of life. Every woman who is anywhere near balanced in the struggle for completeness knows intuitively, that even though she may never beget mortal children, there are innumerable opportunities for the exercise of her maternal functions, awaiting her just behind the veil, which seemingly separates us from invisible areas. Moreover motherhood is qualitative. It is not synonymous with maternity. It is not made nor unmade by the birthrate.

Two important considerations present themselves to the world today: One is that woman—considered as the fecund receptive sex-principle—is refusing the sex relationship on the old basis, however "respectable" and well-intentioned that basis was. Generally speaking, it is evident that the old basis of intercourse between the sexes has been, is being, and will continue to be, disrupted, denied, refused, as the approved and fixed plan and purpose of Destiny. The other important observation is this: there is a cosmic cause for this.

It is only those who are blinded by prejudice or by sense-conscious limitations who refuse to look below the surface for the cause of a condition so general as that of unhappy marriages; of innumerable divorces; of the refusal to bear children. What is the cause? Why are women refusing to marry, or when they do marry refusing to live with their husbands? Why do they shrink from child-birth? Are they less courageous than their progenitors? Or are women less capable of love—either love of children or love of the father who begets the children?

It will be agreed that we are establishing a higher standard of love than ever before in history. We are beginning to realize for the first time in the history of many generations, what we owe to the future. Formerly men built entirely for self, and for the immediate present. We can look back and trace the development of a race consciousness from the clan to the nation. In this century we see the barriers between races and nations and sects and societies, as also between the sexes, slowly dissolving.

Only a few years ago we could not imagine an Oriental, occupying a political, or educational or religions platform with an Occidental. Now it is a common thing. We know the hostility which has existed between the Jew and the Gentile—now they exchange pulpits, and all sects and all nations unite in matters of world interest. Women are elected to political and educational offices. No matter that these evidences of unity are as yet incomplete. They are *promises* of the birth of a larger concept of love than that which prevailed when a man's highest idea of honor and of love was to protect his immediate family only; to care for his own legal wife and children even at the expense of and certainly with heartless indifference to the fate of any other women and children.

To be sure, this protection has often been vouchsafed because of the self interest which is inseparable from the idea of possession and is not, per se, a grander or nobler impulse than that which actuated our hair-clothed antecedents, who found that their own lives were best conserved by respecting those nearest to them. But thus it is that Love has been implanted in human hearts through no higher or more altruistic method than that of self-interest; but the nature of love is to expand; to grow; to *give* of itself until unselfishness must come with the final aim of love, which is *unity* and not possession.

We of this era are unquestionably manifesting a larger and more inclusive ideal of love, and since the Female Principle conserves the higher aspects of love, we are bound to concede that a higher ideal of love is possible to the woman of today than ever before. We must take into consideration the average of the sex, at the same time not forgetting that in the highest type of individual, the qualities of both sexes are balanced, uniting the spiritual, self-sacrificing and unselfish love-element of the female principle, with the wider scope, the inclusive element of the male. Let us remember that we are dealing with principles and not merely with individuals.

Admitting that it is not because of lack of love, either maternal or conjugal, that women are shirking marriage and maternity, we may then ask: "What is the cause?" The answer may be found in the conclusion that women are done with mere instinctive procreation. They demand conditions consistent with the birth of a higher type of human-kind. They desire to "make right the way" for the coming of the perfect race—a race that will not snarl and bite and growl and tear and claw and choke and starve and freeze and otherwise kill each other over the possession of bones.

Ever and ever we have been promised the coming of the perfect man—the "man-god," as Emerson said. This means the God in Man consciously active, and awake. This God-nature of Man's has been asleep, submerged under the domination of the animal nature which subdues and appropriates.

A race of supermen can be born only of full and complete union. Animals reproduce their kind, but man's perogative is to invite the gods to come to earth. We may consciously beget souls, not merely reproduce bodies. Women are demanding a union in which there shall be something more than mere physical contact resulting in reproduction. This demand is working itself out more or less blindly according to the development of individual women, but the ideal of soul union is coming to be more and more recognized not only as a desirable type of union, but also as the initiative of the promised time when the kingdom of God should come on earth as it is in the heavens.

All races have uttered this prayer, apparently with a firm belief in its efficacy. If they have not faith in its appeal, it were surely vain and foolish to voice it But we are assured that "God always keeps his promises," which is simply one way of saying that the law of the cosmos is reliable.

"One calls it Evolution and another calls it God," but both must agree that whether God or Evolution be the name, Love is the result. There can be no higher or more spiritual phase of life than that in which Love is an ever-present reality. Neither can we with any degree of logic assume that a function so universal, so all-pervading, and also so inspiring, as that of Sex, has its beginning and its termination on the physical plane—a manifestation of life which even physicists are bound to concede is an infinitesimal part of cosmic activities.

We need not worry therefore lest the race shall die, because of a decreasing birthrate as we see it on the physical plane. There are many other places and planes of consciousness. The stars and the planets are peopled. The cosmos is very much alive, because Sex is the axis (X-is) upon which it rotates in perfect harmony.

The fact which we here wish to emphasize is that the Female Principle is refusing maternity, and above all the *bondage* of matrimony for the important reason that the time has come for the rearing of the Man-god; for the establishment of the spiritual function of sex, superceding the mere instinctive animal urge of procreation and sense gratification.

Evolution is apparent in all other phases of our life-activities. Why should it not manifest in this most important of all our systems of intercourse?

The mere act of bringing forth children is not in itself either sacred or holy. Far more often it has been a perfunctory duty or a punishment for indulgence in an act of which men and women have been more than half ashamed, even while seeking it with the instinctive urge of a cosmic law which cannot be escaped, although it may be co-operated with to advantage.

Nor does the act of giving birth to children confer true motherhood. Maternity is not necessarily motherhood any more than matrimony is always marriage. There are many mothers who have never borne children. And there are many women with children who know not the first faint dawn of that wonderful, beautiful and intense (because spiritual) love which comes most often in the guise of motherhood, but which is always present when two souls who are truly mated contact each other's inner nature.

If the women of today will insist upon the sacredness and the rightfulness of birth the women of tomorrow will not seek to evade motherhood. If the women of today will establish the sacredness of all life; if they will not rest until every child that is born into this world is recognized as legitimate and more, is welcomed; is given every advantage of education, of healthful body, of right moral training, rest assured that the women of the future will seek only to rival each other in the quality and the perfection of their motherhood.

The efforts of many radicals to enact legislation regulating the birthrate, the struggle to disseminate knowledge of how to prevent conception, may be well meant as these things are consistent with prevailing conditions. But they are not the final answer to the problem. Love is the only answer. Where love is permitted to rule, children are not only welcome but ecstatically desired and provided for.

Motherhood is a hope and a joy to the normal woman. Comparatively every woman would be normal under proper social and economic conditions. When women seek to evade maternity it is either because of lack of sufficient means to care for children, or it is because of lack of sufficient love. Or it is because of fear of that modern mo-loch, Public Opinion.

When a woman truly loves a man, she longs to be the mother of his children. A balanced world will make it possible for every woman to be free from the bondage of fear and poverty, and ill-health, leaving her free to be guided in the most vital and important function of her life, by the call of the highest love of which she is capable. Love will establish motherhood as a divine privilege. Certainly no other power on earth or in the realms above can do so. Neither preachments nor platitudes, nor punishments, nor legislative blunderings. Love is the only saviour of mankind. There is no other true God.

Some day the symbol of Deity which now depicts Man crucified will be superseded upon all altars by the image of a winged babe, and when this comes to pass, Humanity will rise to that ideal.

CHAPTER IV

THE HISTORY OF MARRIAGE AND MATING

Any attempt to discuss subjects pertaining to the sex-relation with intelligence and an optimistic outlook is handicapped by the fact that sex-problems are so intimately associated with religious prejudices, reasons for which we have already mentioned in the chapter devoted to sex-worship and sex-degradation.

It is possible, therefore, that in seeking to define freedom and to make a plea for the freeing of women and men from the "bonds" of matrimony, we may be accused of seeking to demolish with one blow, so to speak, the social institution of marriage.

Such is not the intention of the present writer, for reasons which are based upon something far more noteworthy than a concession to the prejudices and "beliefs" of the average.

Luther Burbank has said: "In pursuing any of the everlasting and fundamental laws of nature, all previous bias and inherited prejudices must be laid aside, if the student hopes to be taken into Nature's confidence and be the sharer of her secrets."

The average person, entrenched behind the bulwark of theological bias, saturated with a belief in the finality of all previous discovery and knowledge, teems with a fanatical desire to "defend his God"—as if the Supreme Power, whatever name we give it—were not capable of self-defense.

It is due to this mistaken zeal on the part of the short-sighted ones, that human evolution is slow, albeit it is likewise inevitable.

They are like those who, viewing the wrecking of a ruined habitation, condemned by the Board of Public Safety, try to stop the process of the workers; they do not know that when the ground shall have been cleared, a finer, more sightly, and above all, more habitable building will be put up on the same ground; and anything from the old architecture that was worthy of preservation will be used in the new building.

The dug-outs of our antedeluvian ancestors were designed to protect them from the destructive forces of storm and wave and also from their brothers, the enemy; and although our ideas of what constitutes a desirable dwelling-place have evolved to our modern ideal of a home, rather than a shelter, yet the fundamental concept remains. A study of history should be encouraging if only to prove that no radical changes in human ethics have ever been forced upon us. Verily, the "gods wait upon men" and until there is something like a concerted demand for improved conditions, they stand just outside the door waiting to be bidden, "Enter, Friend."

As with mental ideas, so it is with ethical ideals. Until there is a more general demand for a higher concept of marriage, it is quite certain that the world will worry along with the one which now does duty for the majority, although it must be admitted that the poor thing gives evidence of much decrepitude and suffers from as many complaints as a hypochondriac.

But, the fact that marriage in some form has prevailed as one of the fundamental necessities of human ethics, ever since the beginning of recorded history, and doubtless before that, is, we believe, very satisfactory evidence that marriage has a permanent place in social and individual evolution. What that place is, can be deduced from a study of the history of marriage.

There are two different viewpoints from which we may discuss all phases of Life, namely, the mystical and the ethical. The mystic sees all life from the inside, as it were; and the physicist studies the exterior, the appearance. To the mystic, the visible, or external, world is a succession of symbols, which he must interpret. To him, the everlasting and fundamental truths of the Cosmos are told in a succession of moving pictures. In fact, the mystic has long anticipated the art which we now see manifested in our film-theatres and has realized that the scenes, which appear to the eye as actual events, are but the reflection of scenes enacted in a place far distant and long before the moment of projection upon the screen which meets his eye.

Science examines, dissects, and classifies these symbols according to their relation to other symbols which the mind has previously noted and classified. The same conclusion awaits both Science and Mysticism.

Humanity is ever seeking the Reality—the Noumenon, which we intuitively postulate as behind the phenomena of Nature.

The institution of marriage, coming down to us through all the ages, side by side with the mystery of sex, and incorporated with the sex-mystery into every form and system of religious rites and ceremonials among all peoples, would seem to have a place in human ethics, as substantial and as permanent as the germ of life itself.

Indeed, the institution of marriage, in its first stages of evolution, obtains in the animal kingdom, where selection in a great variety of forms is common.

And it must be confessed that here we find the same tendency to change and variation, both in regard to the individual and the family species, as we have in the human family.

Polyandry, polygamy, and monogamy, have been general among some animals while among others only one form of mating has been the rule.

Strange to say, sex promiscuity is not at all general among the animals, though polygamy is common. The adoption of polygamy is obviously due to one of two things, or possibly, to be more specific, to both. First, because the percentage of deaths among the males is greater than among the females; this applies to animal life, both wild and domestic. In wild life, because of frequent combats; in domestic life, because the females are kept for breeding while the males are slaughtered for food.

The second reason is because the female is seldom as virile as the male, and to this is also added the debilitating effect of bearing and rearing the young, the necessity for which must have manifested itself very early among the various families, from motives of self-protection, if from nothing higher, since victory evidently favored the numerically strong.

In bird-life, especially, where love is so vital a part of their life, and so beautifully expressed, monogamy is the rule, and in some species, like that of the robin, a certain aristocracy seems to exist, preventing intercourse with any other family. The robin will mate only with a robin, and not infrequently mates for life; which is to say that should one die, the other refuses to mate again.

It is claimed that the bald-headed eagle never varies from monogamy. A mate once chosen, the union lasts until the death of either partner. It does not follow from this, however, that the bald-headed eagle is a creature of a superior moral conscience. It may be that he is guided in his selection of a conjugal mate by an intuitional power undeveloped by other types of life, or, which is far more probable, it may be that his sexual nature is easily satisfied and that he has no temperamental affinities or repulsions, in which event force of habit would be the strongest actuating power. This explanation is in keeping with the eagle character.

The point is that marriage, or what constitutes marriage, exists among birds and animals, and that it antedates history as a social institution among men. Another fact which we must concede, if we are just, is that marriage apparently knows no systematic and upward trend. There is, in fact, no determined evolution toward a definite and conclusive practice of monogamy, although the monogamic custom is recognized as the evolutionary type among the civilized races of today. Nevertheless, it would be folly to imply that a strict monogamy obtains in the letter of the word, or that social exigencies might not reinstate polygamy as a legalized custom.

Passing over those forms of mating, which may be classed as sex-promiscuity, such, for example, as exist among the Esquimaux, and also among the Dyaks, of Borneo, where a "contract" is made for a night by the simple expediency of the man and the woman exchanging head-gear, we come to one of the earliest and most general forms of marriage among primitive peoples, where the parents arranged a marriage between their children for reasons of personal profit. In these instances, neither the youth nor the girl was consulted and generally did not meet until they met to consummate the marriage. In fact, they seemed not to have any preferences. These marriages were easily broken, unless children resulted therefrom, when there seems to have developed a sense of obligation to the offspring to continue the family.

Marriage by capture grew out of the matriarchal system and came as the very natural revolt of the male from the female rule, in which he had no rights and no home with his spouse. Since the gens of the family was the first consideration and this was maintained by the female heads of a clan, there was nothing left for the male to do, if he would be a factor in the community, but to steal his wife from her family, and establish a family life of his own. Thus the female became the possession of the male, by his right of capture and defense.

Inspired by the thirst for further invasions, the male gradually acquired not only one, but many wives, which constituted his "possessions," from the fact that he had earned them by right of conquest, conquest being not only the savage but also the civilized idea of "earning."

Indeed, our modern marriages reveal a degree of savagery in this respect, which is not suspected by the casual observer. The almost general observance of what has come to be known in legal jurisprudence as "the unwritten law," which permits a man to go unpunished when he kills another man whom he believes to have been on terms of intimacy with his wife, is a tacit admission of a man's vested rights in his wife's person.

In innumerable instances, which have been given world-wide publicity within very recent times, the man who has been guilty of homicide under these circumstances has been exalted to the plane of a martyr-hero, and one woman writer, whose hysterical effusions are given considerable space in the public print, defended a man who had taken advantage of this "unwritten law" to shoot his rival, in the following words: "You, Mister, would shoot a man whom you found prowling through your house with the intention of stealing your silver; your jewelry; your property of whatever kind or value. How much more, then, should you guard the honor of your wife, from these pestilential marauders?"

Of course we question the right of human beings to kill each other in defense of mere property; but that is not the point here. The inference here is obvious that this woman, who represents at least the average degree of intelligence, placed her sex in the category of man's possessions, utterly ignoring the woman's right, or power of free-will.

Mention is here made of this incident to show how deeply rooted is the possessive idea of marriage, which had its origin in nothing more ideal than the animal instinct of the dog with the bone.

Nor would we give the impression that this one-sided idea of what constitutes a monogamous marriage is confined to the male. The same idea of possession as of a piece of property, representing so much investment of time and money, and service of one kind or another, actuates the female also although the rights of the woman in the male are not so generally defended and she seldom resorts to such violent methods of defense or of revenge for loss of her property. Perhaps she has a keener sense of values. Necessity has substituted "support" for "outraged honor," and modern woman avenges the loss of her possessions through the safer channels of the law-courts.

The feeling of possession, so ingrained in human nature, and so much a part of our modern marriage relation, is not grounded upon a moral code, which has for its basic principle fidelity to one's partner. This is proven by the fact that men have for some time abrogated to themselves the right of promiscuity, the main clause of their defense being that their conduct does not deprive their wife and family of satisfactory maintenance. Many a woman today, irreproachably respectable and church-going, will admit to herself if not to her neighbors, that she closes her eyes to her husband's laxity in sexual matters, "as long as he provides well for me."

When we come, as we will later, to a consideration of what constitutes morality, we will see that, like all our evolving ideals, it is governed by immediate conditions, both individual and social.

It is easy to see why polygamy has been practiced, as a necessary expedient, and why women have been held so cheaply, when we realize the centuries of devastating wars, both of conquest and of defense, which besmirch the path of Evolution.

Thus the tendency to æsthetic selection, always more pronounced in the female than in the male, has been swallowed up in the false valuation put upon the male, because of his relative scarcity.

In America, in the early sixties, fear of the epithet "old maid" drove many a woman to marriage with a man whom, personally, she did not like, but as he represented a more or less "rara avis" and as her claim to attractiveness rested upon her success in trapping this rare bird, she permitted herself to become a victim of conditions; and we may safely conclude that no higher motive actuated the average woman of the last century than that of submission to conditions, for the "virtues of fidelity and devotion to the home and fireside" which critics of present-day morals are fond of reminding us characterized our grandmothers.

Briefly, then, we may review the history of marriage and of mating, everywhere, and at all times, as variable, controlled by expediency; and always based on the egoistic idea of possession, expressed by the right of the parents to dispose of their children; the right by capture; the right by purchase; and the right by consent.

One or all of these customs have been tried in various parts of the world and at various times, and seldom has the condition of woman approached even so enviable a place as that of the female animal, except in the comparatively short periods when women have been the gens of the family.

These periods have become more and more infrequent, until the legal status of women has been, as it is now, no more than what the evolving consciousness of the male permitted to her.

It is a question whether, under our pretended monogamy, which is, per se, a more ideal condition than polygamy, all women have been either better conditioned or more moral. The answer depends largely upon our idea of what constitutes morality. Certainly, the condition of women in Christian countries has been, and is now, far from ideal; which would, judging from surface appearances, indicate that monogamy, as it has been practiced in the past, served only as an ideal, and at best has been of first aid to the male, primarily because of a question of personal health and cleanliness; secondly, as a means of developing in him the latent qualities of altruism, manifested selfishly enough at first in protecting his possessions; among which he egotistically conceded *his children at least* first place; although the wife was hardly more than a convenience and an incubator.

Of the conditions that have prevailed under the monogamous custom and among the so-called superior races, Letourneau, in his *Evolution of the Family*, says: "The Hebrews seem to have been alone, among the Semites, in adopting monogamy, at least in general practice. Doubtless the subjection of the Jewish woman was not extreme as it is in Kabyle; it was, however, very great. Her consent to marriage, it is true, was necessary when she had reached majority, but she was all the same sold to her husband. We find hardly more than the portrait of a laborious servant, busy and grasping. We shall see that the wife, though she might gain much money, which seems to have been the ideal of the Hebrew, according to the Proverbs, was repudiable at will, with no other reason than the caprice of the master who had bought her. Finally, and this is much more severe, she was always obliged to be able to prove, *cloths in hand*, that she was a virgin at the moment of her marriage, and this under pain of being stoned."

The same state of affairs or worse existed in India and in Persia, although in Persia there seems to have been an attempt to enjoin the same fidelity upon the husband as upon the wife, according to the Zend-Avesta; the only severe restriction to marriage being that neither should marry an infidel. In India, where there has been for centuries an alleged monogamy (except among the privileged classes, where concubinage held sway), the ethical condition of the women has been, and still is, deplorable.

In ancient Greece and Rome the position of the woman was most inferior. She was generally purchased, or given for service. Her husband's word was law, and mothers were compelled to obey their male children as uncomplainingly as though they were slaves. The wife and mother was not permitted to attend festivities and neither was she allowed the selection of her friends, her husband deciding this choice for her.

This, of course, applied to the respectable, or so-called virtuous woman, which constituted the average. Then, as now, two classes of women were to some extent exempt from this rigid custom. One class was formed by those women whose wealth conferred upon them a degree of power, because the possessors of great wealth have always been a law unto themselves. The other class was formed by the women who practiced prostitution, and who, by reason of their mode of life, met men on terms of at least temporary social equality.

Thus it is evident that the path of the virtuous woman without the independence that accompanies the possession of her own money, was in ancient days much more thorny than that of the concubine or the prostitute; and it is because of this fact that parental love, the most powerful of all levers employed by the Cosmic Law to lift love out of degradation, instituted the custom of the "dowry," and although this, too, has at various times become a source of degradation, inspiring impoverished aristocrats to loveless marriages with so-called inferiors, yet it has after all been a factor in the evolution of women and the preservation of the races. It has served two purposes. It has made women, in theory at least, more independent; and it has resulted in an admixture of blood which has saved the aristocratic class from extinction through decadence.

As might well be expected in those instances where women did enjoy a degree of liberty that was due to financial and social advantages, they took a mean delight in ruling it over their male relatives, and, as we may note in our own time, men who yielded to the seduction of wealth, and married women to whom they were forced to accord the freedom and the deference which wealth confers, complained bitterly of their lot; as witness the following complaint of a Roman husband: "I have married a witch with a dowry; I took

42

her to have her fields and houses, and that, O Apollo, is the worst of evils."

One dominant idea controlled the status of marriage in early Greece and Rome—an idea in full accord with the materialistic phase of their civilization; this was the idea of procreation; an idea that logically was inevitable, since continuous warfare resulted in a population in which women predominated, and we are told that in the interest of procreation both childlessness and celibacy were severely punished. Thus the situation of women was that best described by the phrase "between the devil and the deep sea."

Regarding the "ideal of marital fidelity," Plutarch is authority for the story that Cato loaned his wife to his friend Hortensius and took her back on the death of the latter, plus a rich inheritance from the transaction. However, should Martha have yielded herself voluntarily to Hortensius, from motives of affection, the chances are that she would have met death at the hands of her "justly outraged" spouse.

In Europe, similar conditions prevailed, and although monogamy was the rule, concubinage and prostitution in all its forms existed. The wife was subject to the husband in every wish and whim, and after him to the eldest son. This is true today in Germany and among the Saxons in a degree whose modifications do not accord with other advances in our social ethics.

It is a mistake to claim that religious systems have had any direct influence in the emancipation of women during the nineteen hundred years of Christian civilization among the white races.

Religious systems have only reflected the race-thought; they have not molded it. This is true, despite the fact that true religion, when esoterically understood, has always aimed at union, and union means equality along all lines, sex-equality; social equality; race equality.

We must here digress from the main point of this chapter long enough to explain that equality is not synonymous with identity, as seems to be the impression among the many; a misconception which we regret to say is shared by the judge on the bench with the workingman on the construction gang, and the idiotic observation that "if women expect to vote they must expect to stand up in the street-car," is not, alas! confined to the lout, but is quite often voiced by the professional man.

The same silly idea prevails with regard to race-equality. It is judged by a similarity to our own in matters of dress; or choice of foods; by inconsequential differences, rather than by an estimate of what a given race may contribute to the variety of human knowledge; and yet it is evident that nature aims at variety; at a multiplicity of ideas and customs and creations.

43

Differentiation is the primal attempt.

Woman's claim to equality should be based upon the fact that first of all she is different from, rather than identical with, men.

The woman who dons male attire and eschews all so-called "feminine frivolity" in her efforts to prove herself man's equal, is confessing that in her natural environment she does not consider herself his equal, and is masquerading as man, in the vain hope that she may deceive herself and others into thinking she is.

An individual is important to Society in proportion to his originality; in proportion as he contributes some new idea; some hitherto unfamiliar view.

Returning to the point of what constitutes true religion, namely, a consciousness of our unity with all life, we find that although religious ethics have included this ideal, it has not been emphasized in the ratio of its importance. The result is that where unity should have been established, segregation has been the rule, and it is without any desire to reflect discredit upon the ideal of the Church that we point to the fact that woman's emancipation, and her co-operation in all departments of life, as a hope, if not a consummated reality, has but now made its initial bow to the world.

That this initial bow comes side by side with, if not actually in the wake of, disruption of the old theologic dogmas; dissatisfaction with religious systems; and a determined disregard for what has been presented as religion; cannot be denied. The fact is that religious creeds never save anyone; never really elevate nations. At best they have been but a "consolation prize" or a narcotic. Love of freedom is the great liberator.

The influence of Rationalism, as inaugurated by Ingersoll in America and Bradlaugh in England, was the opening wedge. Christian Science, mothered by a woman, incorporated the phrase "Father-Mother-God" into its literature, and unity has been the avowed ideal of all the variety of new cults and philosophies presented under so great a variety of names that we cannot here enumerate them.

Nevertheless, we are still many leagues short of realizing this ideal, despite the preachments in its favor. Politically, the ideal of unity is presented, more or less imperfectly, of course, as Socialism, and Suffrage. Commercially, still more imperfectly in the merchants' "let us get together on this," and in efforts at legislation that shall control corporation dividends and labor schedules, and regulate hours of work. In fact, all along the line we see the shadow cast by the rising sun of unity.

We have thus briefly traced the history of marriage and of mating, in order that we may discuss with sane impartiality the questions: What does marriage symbolize? What is its function in the life of the social body; in the existence of the sphere itself; of the entire Cosmos?

Has it any real place and purpose beyond that of procreation, or any more spiritual function than the perpetuation of the human species?

CHAPTER V

THE SYMBOLISM OF MARRIAGE AND OF SEX-UNION

Notwithstanding the patent fact that the institution of monogamous marriage has not resulted in an ideal condition, it is also plain that any other ideal of sex-union is impossible to a highly developed race.

Monogamy, despite its present unsatisfactory condition, is a promise of the highest ideal to which mortals can aspire; it is the imperfect image of that ideal state which human nature has always striven for. That we have striven for the most part blindly; that we have fallen far short of the ideal aimed at, should not deter us from realizing that the ideal is right.

Monogamy, as a type of the perfect marriage, symbolizes the meeting and the consequent union of a man and a woman who are perfect complementaries.

In order to be a perfect and lasting union, they must be spiritual counterparts. Without this counterpartal affinity as the base of union, no power on earth can force them to unite, although all the laws of men be employed to keep them tied to each other in the body. If two persons belong to each other by the inviolable law of spiritual counterpart, no multitudinous set of man-made laws can keep their souls apart, although these codes may temporarily separate them in the flesh. The bonds of true matrimony are "holy"—the word meaning whole; entire; complete; but these bonds are of an interior nature; they may be judged only from the interior nature of two persons; and any attempt to decide this all-important question from the standpoint of exterior judgment must fail.

The perfect union of the one man and the one woman is the highest ideal of marriage of which we can conceive; but shall we for that reason insist that marriage as a social institution is always complete and holy? When two immature persons come together under the stimulus of no more complementary impulse than the blind force of chemical attraction and cohesion—an instinct, which we share in common with every form of life, from the lowest insect to man—shall they be compelled to abide by that act "as long as they both shall live" in the physical body?

We would say, "Heaven forbid!" only that the appeal is unnecessary. Heaven does forbid, and that is why we see so many attempts to disrupt these immature relationships.

"The striving of sexual elements through affinities, or passional attractions, after congenial marriage unions, is the cause of all the motions, growths, and activities in the physical and moral world," says a writer, and he adds: "The failure to attain the desired end, and the warfare between uncongenial and repulsive elements is the cause of all the broken equilibriums, discords, and collisions in both spheres. If the atomic marriage in nature were perfect, there would be no storms or droughts, or poisons or monstrosities, or disease. If the marriage between the individual will and understanding, between the interior and exterior life, were perfect, we should have regenerated men upon earth, worthy to be called sons of God. If the marriage between the sexes were perfect, we should have a Social Paradise."

Marriage, then, in the sense of the conjugal union of two persons of opposite sex, is the most important function of our lives; every other activity is subsidiary to it. Commerce is carried on, only because of this union; all the laws of man are the outgrowth of marriage; all morality comes from the ideal marriage—the union of Wisdom and Love. To imagine that a function, so vitally important to our exterior life, should have no place in the phases of life which we know as "higher," is a manifest absurdity, and comes from those attenuated concepts of what constitutes spirituality, which Theology has postulated; concepts which, entrenched behind the walls of "thus saith the Lord," have temporarily defied modern progress.

There is no wide gulf between the spiritual and the material worlds, although the material is but an imperfect reflection of the basic principle of life.

Marriage, then, is eternally going on, "Nature is a system of nuptials," says a writer, and nature is only the language of spirit or Divine Life.

How it came about that Theology made the mistake of degrading sex-union and of limiting it to the ephemeral life of the body only, we shall come to later. For the present, a brief resume of the types of marriage ceremony, which have been universal, will convince us that Nature has always sought to convey to the human mind this great secret of eternal and never-ceasing union of complementaries.

Take, for example, the symbol of the wedding-ring. This custom, varying only in unimportant details, consistent with the prevailing social custom of the times, has come down to us from prehistoric days. The golden circle, sometimes worn only by the bride, but frequently by both bride and groom, is emblematical of the completion of the circle of wisdom and the final attainment, in "the twain made one," of the finding by each of "the other half." The circle is always used to express the Absolute; Aum; the Supreme Power that is "without beginning and without end."

According to the old Jewish law, the wedding ring must be made of pure gold and must be earned and paid for by the bridegroom; he might not acquire it by credit or gift. There is in this custom something more than mere thrift; or the assurance of the bridegroom's ability to sustain the needs and comforts of his wife and prospective family. It symbolizes the truth that no one may hope to acquire this priceless blessing of perfect conjugal union, other than by his own efforts. Immortality must be earned, and perfect union, counterpartal union—which means actually "twain made one," comes only by dint of strife and demand and proof of our fitness for the Perfect Life.

Another custom, which has been in almost universal vogue, is that of drinking wine, emblematical of the "wine of life," at the completion of a marriage ceremony. Sometimes this has been the prerogative of the bride and groom only; and sometimes of the officiating priest; but more generally the entire company has shared in this custom. Wine drinking thus symbolizes eternal youth and virility, which can be enjoyed only by those who have attained to the complete life—the divine or spiritual sex-union.

This symbolism is obvious when we take into our consciousness the truth that only complementaries have the power to act and react, without change, or loss. Equilibrium is maintained by a perfect balance of two forces; if one force be ever so small a fraction less than the other, perfect balance is lacking.

Another marriage custom in general use among the ancients was the donning of a crown on the wedding day. This custom formerly included the bridegroom as well as the bride, but later was confined to the bride alone, as was also the custom of wearing a veil. At early Greek marriages crowns made of gold or silver were placed upon the heads of both bride and groom; tapers were lighted; and rings exchanged.

We have a similar custom today in all fashionable church weddings. We have the lighted tapers, signifying the quenchless fires of love; and the circlet which symbolizes eternity.

The crown symbolizes the truth that a truly spiritual union bestows the crown of immortality; the power of Godhood in the Kingdom of Love; which supersedes all earthly kingdoms in splendor. This is a literal truth, although it cannot be understood in its full significance until we are *fit for the kingdom.*

The veil which the bride lifts at the completion of the ceremony symbolizes the truth that when we shall have attained to the spiritual marriage, the veil that separates the interior from the exterior life, shall be lifted; it is so thin that the illusion, of which the wedding veil is made, rightly symbolizes this apparent separation of the physical life from the spiritual. When the veil is lifted, we shall know our completement in the bliss of perfect union; and when we have found that other half of our being, which is the underlying urge of our every thought and act, we shall find the veil lifted. The entire panorama of the universe becomes an open book. There is no "visible" and "invisible;" it is all One, with our own bi-une sex nature for the pivotal center.

So simple and so obvious are all these symbols of the natural man that we are astounded, when we have found the key, that we did not sooner penetrate their meaning. "She will have a crown in Heaven," we say of some self-sacrificing and loving soul, and the phrase suggests to most of us the power of earthly kings and queens with all their splendor of jewels and retainers; but there is an inner meaning which the splendor and the crowns of earth's kings and queens symbolizes.

Spiritual union with the perfect complement of our interior nature is in itself the crown of regal power, of which earthly rulers are symbolical. The spiritual body through this union becomes radiant; luminous; and shines with such splendor that it dazzles the eyes of the beholder. What constitutes the beauty and the value of gems—diamonds; rubies; sapphires; emeralds; topaz; pearls?

It is the radiations of light which they throw off; it is their luminosity—their transparency. It is, indeed, true, that the power which we see exemplified in the rulers of the earth has a corresponding meaning in a spiritual sense; as, in fact, have all things which we cognize with our physical eyes. The Hindus tell us that all things are either the "nita" or the "ita" message. Either they tell us "this is the way to the heights;" or "this is not the way."

The crown of orange blossoms which has supplanted the ancient crown of gold and silver and tinsel, worn with such unconsciousness of its esoteric message, symbolizes one of the most beautiful truths relating to the spiritual marriage—counterpartal union.

Even as this union confers a beautiful radiance upon the spiritual body, the body also becomes sweet-scented like a flower. Weeds, we remember, have no scent or they may be obnoxious in their odor. Weeds are unregenerate flowers.

Certain chemical combinations produce nauseous gases. The human body is a laboratory in which chemical changes are constantly going on. The changes produced by sex-functioning are greater than anything which the experimental chemist has ever discovered in nature.

It is a fact well known to the pathologist that an unwilling wife, however faithful she may be, if forced into the sexual act, may present her husband with a well-defined case of genital disease; nor is this at all strange when we consider the now well-recognized fact that anger, fear, revenge, avarice, and all the destructive thought-forces produce poisons in the secretions of the body.

In Rosicrucian literature, we have the story of "the Chymical Marriage of Christian Rosy Cross," which is, when read with the key to its esoteric meaning, a story of the chemistry of marriage between the sexes. Indeed, the whole story of the secret doctrines of the Rosicrucians, is the story of the sexes, and the "secret of secrets," which was so zealously guarded by the Hermetics and the Rosicrucians and other secret societies, is the secret of the spiritual union of the male and the female principles throughout nature and culminating in man and woman, conferring upon them immortal life through the perfect balance of sex.

It has been said that women were not admitted to the Brotherhood of the Rosicrucians, but this is not true, as there is plenty of evidence to prove.

Owing to the enmity of the established Church toward any exaltation of the sex-relation, and particularly toward the veneration of woman, it became necessary for those who sought to keep alive the fires of Esoteric Wisdom to surround themselves with the most rigid secrecy; in consequence of this, the story of the sexes, constituting the very heart and center of Hermetic philosophy, has been told in allegory, unintelligible unless one has the inner sight or has been initiated into the secret code.

In the sixteenth and seventeenth centuries, the Church had so far succeeded in undermining the work of the Hermetics, that women were excluded from the Brotherhood, and the apparent sole purpose of the secret order was the search for metallic transmutation. Side by side with this convincing evidence that the esoteric meaning of the symbols has been perverted, we find their allegorical phraseology intermixed with frequent allusions to passages from the Scripture and to the Virgin Mary, proving conclusively that the Church, then in the zenith of its power, had confiscated the archives of the secret order, and, either through fear of the influence of their work, or possibly through lack of any adequate comprehension of their wisdom, had employed their symbolism to the further glory of the temporal power of the Church.

This subject will again be dealt with in a chapter devoted to "The Hidden Wisdom," and so we will leave it for the present.

One other great spiritual truth relating to marriage is found in the intimate and constantly recurring association of the turtle-dove with the ceremony of marriage.

The dove is, par excellence, an example of conjugal love. The turtle-dove, more than any other of the dove family, is noted for the fervor of its sexual desires; fidelity to its mate; and for the devotion and diffusion of its love nature. It is well known that if either of a pair of turtle-doves dies, the mate will grieve itself to death. "Like a pair of turtle-doves" is said of a couple who are happily married, and the domestic life of the dove has made the dove a symbol of peace.

Doves have been held sacred in many parts of the world, and figure prominently in religious symbolic architecture and utensils, from ancient times down to the present day. The symbol of the doves flying over the ark of the covenant typifies the spiritual origin of birth, the ark being the primordial egg, from which issued all the forms of life. Let us also remember that they issued *in pairs*.

CHAPTER VI

CONTINENCE; CHASTITY AND ASCETICISM; THEIR SPIRITUAL SIGNIFICANCE

From the earliest forms of sex-worship, in which the creative function was doubtless given its rightful place, down through successive stages of sex-degeneracy, we come to the sex-perversions and the almost general licentiousness of Ancient Greece and Rome, with whom the sex function became nothing more exalted than a method of procreation, in common with the animals; and a means of sense-gratification, on a par with gluttony.

Even among the intellectual Greeks, the highest type of a civilization that, although epicurean and esthetic, was yet essentially materialistic, sexual intercourse had no more spiritual place than it occupies today in fine stock-breeding.

Between ancient Roman licentiousness and our own modern attitude toward the sex-relation, there intervenes that terrible time in the history of Human Evolution, known as the Dark Ages, in which was evolved the unnatural view of the function of sex, exemplified rather erotically, in many instances, by asceticism and celibacy. Although it sounds paradoxical, yet there is a celibacy that is distinctly erotic.

In reading of some of the experiences in the lives of the saints, the normal, healthy person feels an aversion similar to that which he experiences in viewing the effects of physical disease; and yet we must note in this abnormal attitude of the Church toward the sex-relation, the effect of nature's attempt at equilibrium; a revulsion from the effect of the centuries preceding.

Some of the contributing causes of this revulsion were: celibacy, except within the Church, forbidden by the Roman Senate; the fact that women had no choice in marriage; the devastating wars which took the best of physical manhood; and the cheapness of women, every man of wealth having as many slave women as he could house and feed; the orgies where women, both bound and free, were openly debauched; all these evidences of the utter degradation to which the pure and beautiful function of sex had sunk, called for a revulsion; and it came in the idea of asceticism—an instance where the remedy was worse than the disease. The mental attitude that resulted in asceticism was not one in which the sex function was lifted from the mire of licentiousness in which it lay; rather it was abandoned altogether as something vile and unclean; and that too, unhappily, by those who should have known better.

The Roman Church, in full accord with the type of Roman mind which fostered it, still harbored the perverted idea that women were inferior. And it is from the Roman Church of today rather more than from any other of the phases of Christian Orthodoxy, that we note a militant opposition to woman suffrage, and all the other avenues of woman's claim to free expression.

While retaining all the old Roman's disrespect for woman, the Church instituted and fostered celibacy, as a way out of the old profiligacy, but as though by a sort of spiritual irony, the Church has retained, from its "pagan" ancestors, the sex-worshippers, the idol of the Holy Virgin. And despite the bombardments of criticism from without and the inculcation of superstitious ignorance from within, the pure-hearted children of the Church have always gone to the "Holy Mother" for their comfort; and thus the eternal fires of Truth have smouldered beneath the ashes of perverted mysticism throughout the Dark Ages that are gone and the scarcely lighter Dawn that is here. Those who have eyes to see, realize that the one worth-while thing which the old, nearly-blind Church has been unwittingly doing all the time, has been to hold to this central truth of all Life—religious, social, national, and domestic—the truth that it is only by exalting the maternal function of human life, that we can hope to reach the saviour of mankind.

And, lest there be still some misconception of what we consider to be the true "saviour" of mankind, we will again state, even as the Church itself states it, "the babe of Bethlehem"—the pure Love between one man and one woman; the "twain made one," which is the only saviour that ever was or ever will be —the pure Christ-child that is born of conterpartal union.

Let those who would cling to the idea of an individual man, born in a city called "Bethlehem" as the saviour of the world, remember that even so, the city derived its name from the word, "bethel," meaning a pure white stone, rounded at the top, in exact imitation of the omphalos of Apollo, in the temple of Delphi. And when the shock of his discovery has somewhat subsided, and his prejudices have been swallowed up in a desire for the whole Truth, let him remember also that this central idea has been the foundation of all religious rites since time began; and instead of feeling that the whole fabric of Christianity has been rent by the light of scientific discovery, he will see that it has merely been *revealed*, and the revelation will prove to him that Truth is the most beautiful, the most spiritual and the most satisfying thing in life, because the Truth is that Perfect Love is the only passport to immortal bliss. No one can withhold Heaven from us, if we have this perfect love.

Thus the essentials of Christianity are the essentials of every other religious system; and the essentials are: Love is the One true and only God; and Sex is the form in which this Bi-une God appears; according to our individual and collective reverence for this bi-une God, will be our spiritual development.

We do not reverence sex when we cheapen it by dissipation; or when we abandon it as unclean and unworthy and unholy; both attitudes are abnormal, and unbalanced.

Spiritual consciousness aims at equilibrium. The perfectly balanced person is equally developed on all planes; the perfectly balanced individual, in sufficient numbers, will produce a balanced and therefore a healthy social organization; and a balanced and healthy-minded race of beings will result in a balanced sphere; this fact is foreshadowed by the postulate which Science is now considering, to wit: the earth's axis may be straightened, and, if so, a uniform temperature will prevail on this globe.

Returning to a consideration of the subjects which head this chapter, we find it necessary to clear the ground a little, in regard to a definition of words.

The word continence should apply to the act of self-restraint in the matter of the emotions, desires, and passions, whether of the sex-passion or the passion of anger, avarice, or gluttony. The word has come to mean, in many cases, the total abstinence from the sex-relation, because of the general idea which has prevailed, that any indulgence of sex-love was a confession of weakness. In fact, our modern ideas regarding this subject are so chaotic and so manifestly paradoxical that they are absurd.

On the one hand we have a tradition that motherhood is a beautiful and holy thing; on the other, we regard the sex-relation, per se, as an indecent thing, or at best as a weakness of the flesh.

We have the obvious demonstration that creation is possible only because of the conjunction of the two sexes, and yet we are taught that sex-love is something which is permitted to us in this lower state of our being, and denied in heaven, and at the same time we are told that God creates everything, and God dwells in Heaven, where there is no such "polluting sin" as sex-love.

We certainly do need balance.

The word chastity conveys to the mind (and this is not confined to the undeveloped person, but is general) the idea of a woman who is devoid of the sex-impulse. Chastity, like the word virtue, suggests to our minds no relationship to the character, or inner nature of a person; it has come to be applied to the physical anatomy, and we are not surprised when we realize that the word is seldom used in connection with the male. It is strictly a female attribute—nay, we may almost say, "organ."

If a woman, for any reason whatsoever, whether through lack of opportunity; through hereditary causes; or through repression, or—which occurs more frequently—as a commercial expediency, believing that her person will thus bring more in the matrimonial market—if, as we say, for any reason, however sordid, a woman escapes bodily sex-contact, she is called "chaste" and her "virtue" is extolled.

This is, of course, not a far cry from the ancient days when a bridegroom had the right to turn the bride away from his door, should the evidence of her virginity be lacking; whereupon the poor creature was stoned to death, a sacrifice on the altar of Egoism, the arch-enemy of both sexes.

And although it seems a long, long time from that day to this, we may look back over the Ages, and see the thread unbroken, connecting the Past with the Present; uniting the women of those days with their sisters of today; and we find the answer to this far-off outrage upon the spiritual function of sex, in the horrors of our white slavery, among which horrors, the greatest is not alone the barter and sale of that which should be recognized as sacred, but the perversions, the deceptions and the subterfuges which it entails. One instance, related by a trained nurse who had been in attendance upon a girl sixteen years of age, will suffice to illustrate this. The girl, encouraged by her mother, related with amusement and satisfaction, how the child had "sold her virtue" on seven different occasions, procuring for the same, proven by the requisite evidences, sums which were considered quite exorbitant in view of the fact that the market was always over-crowded with similar sales.

Thus, the law of supply and demand is ever preserved; and human beings keep right on selling their royal birthright for a mess of pottage; inviting disease, decay and death when they might have glorious, blissful life.

Mankind has failed to look for virtue in the interior nature; failed to look for beauty of soul, being ever ready to pay the highest price for the counterfeit, and the result is that a practice of mutual deception has been the rule.

Some years ago, Thomas Hardy wrote a story about a girl in the wretched environment of middle-class England. He called it the story of a "pure woman," and his appraisal of the heroine as a pure woman brought out a storm of reproach and horrified criticism, particularly from the clergy, because it chanced that this poor girl had given birth to a child out of wedlock; and notwithstanding that the author made it quite clear that she had been the victim of circumstances and coercion, the act itself condemned her to unchastity in the eyes of the clerical critics.

When we contemplate the attitude which religious systems have ever held toward women, we are amazed that the Church has been upheld almost wholly by the female sex. The fact is accountable on one hypothesis only: that of the spiritual insight, which recognized in the story of the Holy Mother and the Child the *One primordial, and indestructible key to salvation*—the birth of the god-man through the recognition of the purity and joy of the perfect sex-union.

But, notwithstanding the medieval trend of religious mysticism (there is a religious mysticism and a scientific mysticism) which seemed to regard all human love as a weakness, when not actually sinful as in sex-love, it is evident that sexual love, in its emotional, or psychic aspect, was at the root of the "ecstacies" which are so ardently described in ecclesiastical history as "evidences of saintliness."

If, instead of indignantly denying this fact, as though it were profane criticism of the saints, defenders of the Theological view of mysticism would calmly consider and accept the evidence, they would be able to infuse into the creeds, the vitality which they so lack.

The lives of the saints, in so far as they relate to trance and ecstatic visions, must, sooner or later meet one of two fates. Either they will be analyzed and presented, with the reverence that is due the subject, as proofs of the spiritual function of sex-love; or they must be relegated to the position to which the Church assigns all sexual desire—that of eroticism and innate and ineradicable depravity.

Viewed in the light in which Theology has held the sex relation, the paroxysms which are ascribed to St. Catherine of Sienna, and to the Holy Mechthild and other saints, have in them something decidedly obnoxious; while, if we take the premise that these saints, by virtue of prayer, aspiration, and intended sacrifice of the mortal self to an ideal, transmuted their sex-nature from the physical to the spiritual, then indeed, we have an approach to a mighty truth, which is at once both explanatory and satisfying. St. Catherine is referred to as "the mystic bride;" and Jesus Christ, to whom she was "espoused" (using the terminology which the Church prefers, as suggesting a less physical union than the word "married") was the "bride-groom;" more than that; she declared that she was married with a ring, set with precious stones; just like any other betrothal or wedding ring.

Always in these recitals we find the phraseology which lovers employ when exalting the loved one above the world. The term "My Beloved" is singularly universal, and seems to spring involuntarily to the lips of the lover when his love is of the quality that reverences; adores; and exalts its object. And it is equally foreign to the lips of the dilettante lover.

To their credit be it said, the love which the saints developed within themselves, by dint of their attempts to exalt celibacy in an age of sexual profligacy, is none the less human love; it is human love spiritualized, exalted, and transmuted from the plane of the animal to that of the soul. This transmutation is in fact responsible for the intensity, the absorbing power of the love which thrilled them into such an ecstacy that in most instances they became lost in the bliss of the emotions excited by the inward flow of their sex nature, and were totally unfitted to take part in the outer, or so-called practical life.

Such, for example, was Saint Teresa, of whom William James, in his "Varieties of Religious Experience," says: "Her idea of religion seems to have been that of an endless amatory flirtation—if one may say so without irreverence—between the devotee and the Deity." Although this estimate of St. Theresa's saintliness will doubtless be shocking to the people who think they are pious, we take an optimistic view of it, and suggest that the saint's idea of religion is far more satisfying than that usually presented as saintliness. St. Theresa, like most of the female saints, became "the bride of Christ"—the *man* Jesus, the Christ, let it be remembered.

St. Gertrude, a Benedictine nun of the Thirteenth Century, gave herself up so wholly to this inward contemplation; to fasting, prayer, and withdrawal from the outer to the inner life, that she lived as the "bride of God," in such daily contact with Him as would fitly describe any love-mated honeymoon of today. According to her testimony "God" indulged in such language and caresses, and intimacies, kisses and compliments as would satisfy any woman married to her ideal lover.

In the case of St. Louis of Gonzaga, it is significant that he selected the Virgin Mary as the object of his adoration and "consecrated to her, his own virginity;" and we read how "burning with love, he made his vow of perpetual chastity." In consequence of this vow, he was never tempted as was St. Anthony, by visions of beautiful women.

Here again we have the love of the male for the female. If it were not so, St. Louis may well have chosen Jesus, or Joseph, or John, as the object of his devotional contemplation; and St. Catherine, and Theresa, and Mechthild might have paid their homage to the Virgin Mary.

"Jeanne of the Cross" held constant converse with her guardian angel, who by the way was a beautiful youth, "more brilliant than the sun and with a crown of glory on his head."

St. Frances was inseparable from her angel, whom she loved with extravagant and blissful devotion, and whom she also described as "a young man of such radiant beauty and purity that he melted her soul."

The truth is that, in seeking to escape from the "sin" of human love, as seen in the world, in the union of the sexes, they touched the very main-spring of their sex-nature, intensifying to a degree unknown to the merely sense-conscious person, the ecstatic bliss of spiritual sex-union.

Naturally the question will arise as to whether these saints really came into contact with their spiritual mates in these paroxysms of holy fervor, and if so, why did the vision of the Christ so frequently appear to them and not alone the vision of some other being?

The answer is found in the fact that spiritual experiences must be interpreted through the channel of the outer mind, which in these instances was obsessed by the thought implanted by Medieval Theology, that human love is sinful. It may be questioned whether, even though the visions did relate to some person other than the members of the Holy Family, the fact would have been admitted since it would have been attributed to unworthiness on the part of the saint.

They were practically compelled to include God and Christ in their ecstacies to prove their respectability.

One phrase, commonly employed to describe the kind of love which "flooded the soul" in these saintly ecstacies, is particularly applicable to the effects of spiritual sex-union, as described by those who have experienced counterpartal union, and which Swedenborg so constantly emphasizes in his recital of "conjugal delights." This phrase is "melting love." It is a feeling of melting or merging into the other's being, until there seems to be but one person, formed by the two souls. In fact, it is *union*; whereas the lesser, or we may say the lower, phase, of the sex-relation is at best but *contact*.

If this view of the trances and ecstacies described in the lives of the saints, be repulsive to our readers, we can only say that we are sorry for our readers. They have imbibed the spirit of the Dark Ages, which regarded human love as sinful, overlooking the fact that all we may know of the "love of God," is by analogous comparison to what we know of human love.

If human love be sinful, by logical deduction we would inevitably arrive at the conclusion that the universe is all sinful. In which event, the very word itself would have lost its significance.

The objectionable part of the orthodox view of the effects of saintliness lies in the realization that neither the saints themselves, nor the Church which perpetuates their recitals, had any conception of the real situation, so evident to the enlightened and unprejudiced reader. And if this view of saintly ecstacies, postulating the transmutation of sex-force into spiritual channels, be objectionable, what can be said of the only other view which is possible in the light of the evidence submitted?

Our ideas of what constitutes chastity need revising, else we must needs decide that chastity is more a vice than a virtue.

For example, consider the character of a mother of the self-sacrificing, noble type, devoting her life to the welfare of the human family; interesting herself in all the problems that affect the generations to come; patient; sweet and wise. Compare her with an unmarried girl whose body is immune from contact with one of the opposite sex, but whose mind is bent upon self, and self-adornment; upon the necessity of capturing a wealthy husband, as a means of this self-gratification, without regard to any sentiment or even common affection. Who is the more chaste?

Coventry Patmore says:

"Virgins are they before the Lord,

Whose souls are pure. The vestal fire

Is not, as some mis-read the Word,

By Marriage quenched, but burns the higher."

If purity of soul were synonymous with celibacy, the entire constantly-copulating cosmos would have long since been demolished; but despite the mistaken attitude of religious systems toward the divine function of sex, Humanity is reaching a higher and purer conception of love. As we approach a higher type of civilization, the broader, deeper, and more intense becomes our capacity to love. The more spiritual we become, the more vital is our love-nature, and our love-nature is grounded in sex. Let us not imagine that spiritual love is less sexual than is physical love. Spiritual love is physical love, *plus* all the other phases of love.

The real objection to sex love on the physical plane is not based upon its strength, but upon its weakness. If it be nothing deeper than an attraction of chemical affinities generated by physical activities, it has no reservoir from which to draw its supply. It is like the electrical wire that is "short circuited," it expends itself in one spasmodic combustion.

True spirituality is attained by a process of addition. The common and erroneous idea of spiritual attainment involves a process of subtraction.

We need go no further than to review the processes in the external world of today to understand this fact of the inclusiveness of the spiritual life, in contradistinction to the generally accepted idea of exclusiveness which is attached to a contemplation of the so-called "spiritual."

All our activities are now carried on upon a gigantic scale. Where formerly a little stream supplied the water to the mill, we now harness the invisible and apparently inexhaustible forces of electricity; where formerly commerce was a system of bartering between two single individuals, it is now a huge network involving millions of persons. Everything teaches us the lesson of inclusiveness, as we approach a more spiritualized ideal of life. We are uniting; merging; drawing within.

The Centripetal force of the planet itself, corresponding to the female pole of the magnet, is today the active principle in external life. The machinist knows this when he is compelled to avoid the suction currents of electrical power. Cosmic reaction has set in, and union between complementaries is the result. Applying this truth to individual human life, and we have what?

Counterpartal Sex-union.

CHAPTER VII

SOUL-UNION: WHERE WILL IT LEAD?

We have heard much in recent years of "affinities," and "soul-mates," and we are likely to hear much more in the future. So much that is unsavory and sensational is associated with these two words, that we almost hesitate to employ them; but that is always the way with Fear. It builds a high wall between us and Truth, and dares us to scale it.

We accept the challenge.

To begin with, the words are not synonymous, although frequently used as such. Affinities are based upon mutual interests; mutual tastes and appetites; mutual stages of development; but these stages of development may be sense-conscious only; or they may be of a highly intellectual order. Whatever their basis of mutuality, they tend to attract upon that plane. Whenever this affinity, established by virtue of mutual tastes, is on the sense-plane only—that is, when it is because two persons both like their roast-beef rare; or their whiskey diluted; or their wine iced—we are apt to find the result in a mistaken idea of sexual affinity, which wears itself out for the reasons already stated, because there is no reservoir from which to draw. The chemistry of the body changes with time and emotional experiences. Affinity of bodily contact only, resulting from a congeniality of sense-appetites, is therefore necessarily short lived.

Affinity of intellect is much more lasting, because it approaches a state higher in the ascent to the spiritual center of the cosmos.

Thought is the parent of speech, or of any external appeal to the senses. Back of all objectivity is the thought that molded it; but back of thought is desire; and back of desire is design—cosmic design we may say—expressing itself discretively; in individuals.

Affinities that are based upon intellectual similarities are of a finer nature and generally more lasting than those of sense-conscious attraction only; and it is no uncommon thing to find two persons of the opposite sex enjoying a protracted friendship or preference for each others' society which deceives the average on-looker into thinking that there is also sexual affinity, when as a matter of fact there may never have been any thought of such relationship.

A few brilliant women in former times, notably Madame de Stael, or Margaret Fuller, have enjoyed the attentions and apparent devotion of men for many years without having entered into any more intimate relationship with them.

But these examples have been few in the past, and have been much commented upon. In the present, such desirable companionship is becoming much more common and a woman may now be seen twice with the same man without having the neighbors speculating as to a suitable name for the baby.

More and more, as women become freed from the necessity to "settle themselves" in marriage, we find evidences of this intellectual affinity between the sexes; and more and more, as we get away from the old thought that a man has but one desire, that of sexual intercourse, and a woman but one motive, that of enslaving man through his sexual appetite, we will find that men and women will meet on the plane of intellectual affinity and not be driven by gossip of outsiders, or by the force of the race-thought in their own minds, into seeking to spoil such companionship by a matrimonial alliance, when nature did not intend it to be so.

A number of years ago, when even the little freedom which human beings now accord each other in this matter was denied the struggling sexes, a certain man and woman, who were intellectual companions, married. He was a writer; she was a physician; which is evidence in itself of a degree of intellectual power not so common at that time as now; she was moreover an unusual woman in many ways. They parted after a month of married life and to the horror and scandal of the entire community, remained friends. The scandal reached the climax of disapproval and shocked morality when the man, married again, continued his friendship with his former wife and later, when a baby came to the couple, the ex-wife and mutual friend was the attending physician.

The old idea of matrimony held that the husband and wife must be "yoked" together, so that neither one could exercise any individual predilection or choice of friends, or recreation, or taste or desire. And this is still the average idea of a successful marriage. It is an idea that is not confined to the ignorant, and the narrow-minded. It is the attitude of society at large, though upon what argument such an idea is based, must be left to the perverted imagination.

Presumably it is because of that colossal egotism which insists upon personal ownership. One would expect this tendency to own each other to have died with the death of the institution of slavery, but it still exists, and as we have already observed, among those who sit in the seats of the mighty as well as among the ignorant.

A couple who had married on the ground of intellectual affinity lived together most congenially for a period of twelve years, although they agreed that sexual affinity was lacking in their relationship. They agreed that there was another phase of mating, and that should either come to the point where freedom was desirable, it would be given without resentment or anger. They both decided, that perfect candor and honesty with each other on this score was a higher type of civilization than that which prevails where mutual deceit is the rule.

True to their compact, when the wife met the one whom she believed to be the one man who answered the call of her soul, the husband gave her up, retaining her friendship, and the memory of an intellectual companionship unmarred by the horrors of dispute and deceit and disruption. But he incurred the severest criticism from Society, which is as yet composed of the animal-man, rather than the man-god, and the animal-man (meaning woman as well) knows no higher code of morality than that which he vaingloriously terms "defense of his honor." By exactly what process of reasoning a man can imagine his honor defended or appeased by shooting his rival, is, we admit, beyond our power to fathom. But such is the basis of the unwritten law, in which civilized man vents his remaining savagery.

Affinity-marriages, then, are not synonymous with soul-mating. And while we contend that affinity marriages, based upon at least some degree of mutuality, are a step higher in social development than were the alliances of the old regime, where a man's social or domestic exigencies required a wife or a housekeeper, or both-in-one; where woman must marry whomsoever asked her, or be pitied and scorned as an "old maid," still affinity-marriages are not the final union, and must go through an evolutionary phase.

Affinity-marriages are eligible to disruption. Happily, we trust, these disruptions will in the course of time be devoid of hatred and mutual recriminations and abuse. Certainly they will be, as they evolve from the plane of sense-consciousness to that of intellectual affinities. Moreover, they stand a much better chance of permanency than has maintained during the past, before the word affinity was heard so frequently as it is now.

The general impression is abroad in the land, that it is only since women became economically independent that disruption of the marriage bonds has become so general. It is true that divorces are much more frequent since women have become, to a great extent, economically independent; but that only means that the parties to the marriage have been set free. The disruptions are not more, it is only the evidences. And it is at the *evidence* of marital unhappiness that all the criticism is directed.

If the criticism were directed against the condition that divorce tells us of, instead of against the divorce itself, the first aid to the injured would be to establish a social order wherein an equal moral standard for both sexes should be the rule, and where a mother is recognized, and respected and honored in the name of motherhood, whether she is a wife or not.

This suggestion will of course be met with a shocked gasp from many. The cry that "Society will be disorganized" and our "moral code become chaotic" will go up from the self-constituted keepers of public morality. But is our morality so tender that it needs protection? Are our social conditions so ideal that they cannot be improved? If they are, then nothing can besmirch them. If they are not, they must first be demolished, before they are rebuilt.

The limited mortal mind is always terribly afraid of a change. Not one single improvement has ever been suggested, from mechanics to morals, that has not been met with that ever-ready fear-thought, that the whole universe is going to the eternal bow-wows, if the slightest change in established institutions is made. And despite it all, we go on year after year, improving. "Self-improvement" is the watch-word of the Century. If "self-improvement," then social improvement. Mankind is still in the making, as far as external conditions are concerned.

The complaint goes up from every side, that women refuse motherhood. Girls who have been carefully reared, brought up in the most orthodox movement, are heard to openly, unashamed, announce their intention of finding a rich husband and not, emphatically, *not* having any children.

May this not be Nature's revenge upon our inhuman treatment of girls who become mothers without first becoming wives?

We are wont to refer to unmarried mothers as "unfortunates" and "ruined." But in what does the misfortune consist, and wherein are they ruined?

Is a woman ever unfortunate if she gives birth to a child because she has loved, and because she loves the child? Is she ruined in any way except that she becomes the target for our inhumanity; our well-nigh unforgivable stupidity?

The world, and especially women, owe a debt of gratitude to a certain famous woman who, by her force of character; her defiant self-respect in the face of social criticism, because she had a child and no husband, has wrung from the unwilling public the highest place accorded any actress in this or any previous age. This artist's well-known reply to an openly expressed criticism of her is worthy of perpetuation. "Ah, so!" she said, "true I have a son and no husband, but you women have husbands and lovers, and no children!"

We would not have it understood that we commend this woman's example, and criticise that of the woman to whom she referred. We do not regard child-bearing as the end and aim of woman's mission. It has been said that the first duty of Man is to perpetuate the species, but observation should convince us that in all too many instances the first duty of the individual would be to refrain from such a crime against posterity.

We neither criticise nor advise the adoption of the position of a husbandless mother; nor that of the women who are childless wives. We endorse any woman's insistence upon her right to self-respect; and we insist that a better civilization cannot come without permitting the greatest degree of personal liberty in matters pertaining to the sex-relation, and, above and beyond all, without conceding to the unmarried mother the same respect that we accord to the married one, when she is otherwise worthy of our respect. It certainly takes courage for a defenseless woman to bear a fatherless child, in a hypocritical world.

The normal woman does not live who would not rather be safely and happily married to the man whom her soul tells her exists somewhere in the universe, than to be battling with the problem of existence, alone. When she is so married, we need not fear that the marriage will be disrupted. Until she is so married, no power on earth can, and no power in Heaven will, prevent the disruptions, although man's laws may temporarily obstruct the evidence of such disruption.

What we have already said will make it clear, that our contention is that affinities are not necessarily soul-mates; that, in fact, we may have many and various kinds of affinities, but no one can possibly have more than one soul-mate.

Mates are two entities composing a pair. They are the two halves that make a whole. Unlike what we know of affinities, they are not merely similar; nor yet opposite, so that they attract each other because of curiosity or dissimiliarity.

They belong to each other because together they complete a perfect balance. Each supplies in the exact proportion required for balance the qualities lacking in the other.

In the event of such union, instinctive procreation will cease, and re-generation will begin. They will consciously beget souls, instead of merely providing bodies for souls to manifest upon this external plane of consciousness.

Bodily contact is not essential to this phase of sex-union, because the real conjunction is between the interior natures; and the interior nature exists independently of the physical organism.

Already the race-thought is beginning to realize interiorly. This is manifest in the daily press; in music and drama; and in all the avenues of the senses. That intangible, elusive but potential thing called "character" forms the gist of editorial advice. Everywhere we note a tendency to look below the appearance of things, and to fathom the depths of psychological analysis. For the first time in centuries the race-thought seeks the underlying cause for specific effects, instead of, as heretofore, being satisfied to deal with effects only, suppressing those that are unpleasant and extolling those that seem agreeable.

The scientist expresses it thus: "Nature is giving up her secrets to man." The metaphysician puts it this way: "The soul of man is unveiling, and soon we shall know each other in Truth." The religionist has long looked for a time when, as prophesied by St. Paul, who was above all things a spiritually-conscious person, "we shall see each other face to face; not as now through a glass, darkly."

This tendency to "get behind the scenes" as it were, to penetrate the crust of mere outward semblance, and to reveal the interior nature, may be seen even in the fashions of our clothes. Despite thunders of denunciation from the self-constituted keepers of our morals, who are not yet free from the bondage of traditional ideas of virtue and "respectability," women have insisted upon freedom of the body in dress until at last the uncorseted, short-skirted, thinly-clad woman excites little adverse comment. The fact has at last established itself that the female form has legs.

This fact was only half suspected before; men have always wanted to see exactly what was beneath those long flowing skirts; and woman has always known that she possessed at least one trump card, in the game of enslaving man to become what modern slang has so aptly labeled her "meal-ticket." She could always keep him guessing as to whether or not she had legs; and the average man, be it known, possesses a fund of curiosity far in excess of that which is proverbially ascribed to woman. Men have been known to pay the highest price, even to donning the matrimonial yoke, to satisfy their curiosity. Women have always known this, and the worldly wise mother has besought her marriageable daughter to "keep her skirts well over her ankles" if she hoped to secure a man as a permanent banker! It does sound crude expressed thus, but this is the basis upon which at least nine-tenths of the respectable marriages of society are consummated. And this is the standard which the short-sighted keepers of public morals would have us retain. They would force women to act as though their bodies are vile. They would keep the mind encumbered with the corpse of an idea of modesty, from which the spirit has long since fled. The spirit has fled from it because it was a false idea of modesty; because it was founded upon the idea that woman was an instrument of the devil himself, and that to look upon her naked form was in itself wicked, and only permitted to poor man as a concession to his own innate defilement.

The good Church at one time, not so far distant, refused to admit women to the communion table in the "holy sacrament." A fine chance has any sacrament of being holy, with one half of it missing!

The old idea of womanly modesty consisted of blushing with shame and embarrassment if by chance her ankles became exposed to the interested and curious gaze of a male. Notwithstanding this ideal of modesty, the designing and beguiling female managed to arrange just such a contretemps every time there was an eligible male within sight; if discovered, she either assumed a look of infantile innocence, or she took the opportunity to coax a becoming blush.

To be sure, this does not accurately describe all women of "the good old days." There was the other type.

Nature manifests in extremes. There was the type, fitting ancestors to those women of to-day who are outraged and shocked at the present-day fashions, which actually disclose the fact that women are anatomically endowed with legs and hips, quite in defiance of man's inherited predilection for making this discovery under conditions that would pamper to his satiating sex-appetite. They, poor creatures, were dreadfully ashamed of being women, and they did all that was possible to conceal the fact. They, doubtless, would gladly have amputated their legs, if the ministers had so decreed, and they apologized to the world every time an unforseen circumstance uncovered a portion of these offensive legs. In fact, they denied the existence of "said members," and alluded to them tentatively and with modest hesitation, as "limbs."

"But," some will exclaim, "we cannot see any possible connection between a regenerated race, and a fashion which permits the display of the female figure upon the public streets, where men who are as yet un-regenerated, and licentious, may leer and pass vile remarks, and suggest lustful thoughts."

Few can see any connection between our so-called practical, everyday life, and the spiritual life. They look upon the spiritual life as something remote; something in the dim and ever and ever distant future. The spiritual life is supposed to be so negative that we postpone living it, as long as we possibly can; and whereas the human family has prayed and prayed, for Lo! these many ages: "Thy kingdom come upon earth," they apparently have not had the slightest idea that God would take them at their word.

They are like the old darky who called upon "de Lawd to strike him dead if he was not telling the truth," when as a matter of fact he was lying roundly. At that moment a bricklayer on the building above where Rastus was standing, dropped a brick, which struck the old darkey on the head, and he exclaimed "What's de matter, good Lawd, caint you'all take a joke?"

The Kingdom of God, from all records, whether orthodox or heterodox, has been described as the abode of angels; and angels have been pictured as nearly nude as our silly "morality" would permit. No one has as yet suggested that we compel the angels to wear hoopskirts, although "September Morn" has been compelled, by police regulation, to don a sweater.

The spiritual life awaits our cognizance, just behind the transparent veil of our limited mortal consciousness. This is the message of the "unveiling" of the female form. This is the time of woman's revealment of true modesty; true ideals. The Female Principle, representing the spiritual element in nature, hitherto shut in; covered up; hidden—is coming out.

Men must learn to be able to look upon the female form without spasms of either lustful desires; or contemptuous indifference.

There was a time when the presence of a female office-force in the business section of a city was the signal for unwarranted familiarity on the part of some of the male members of a corporation. There was a time, when women first invaded the ranks of the "down-town" business centers, that a woman's appointment to a responsible position rested upon her claims to feminine attractiveness. Now, the only question asked is, "Is she efficient?"

That which she is, in her interior nature, is the final test of her power. When men have become inured to the knowledge, so long concealed, that women have legs and that there is no more seductiveness in them than in their faces, the love of man for woman will undergo the same evolution that his estimate of her business efficiency has undergone. He will judge her by what she is in her interior nature; and his sexual desires, now manifested distractedly in mere love of the female, will become concentrated in love of the one woman to whom his soul turns in irresistible sex-attraction, as unerringly as the needle turns to the pole to which it is magnetized.

Is this fact so unmanifest? Does not everything point to it?

A few years ago, a man and a woman could not pass a day together in mutual conversation, and interest, without encroachment upon the one emotion which they were supposed to hold in common—sexual attraction.

That was indeed the whole sum and substance of communication between the two sexes, if we may except the rare instances which history has made much of, because of their rarity—women of the French salons, who have become famous for their wit and beauty, in neither of which attributes did they outstrip the average self-supporting woman of today.

But custom has slowly, but perceptibly, established the possibility of a frank and non-sentimental companionship between the male and the female, and the result is that both are much more clear as to the true character of their sentiments toward each other. Neither is blinded by the force of undifferentiated sex-attraction.

There must be some specific basis of mutual love; hence we have the vogue of the "affinity," and by the term is instantly recognized a special force of attraction, independent of undifferentiated sex alone. It is known that there is at least an assumption of an interior attraction, and we insist that affinity marriages, however incomplete as yet, are still superior in motive to that of mere marriage, where it is a case of *a* male and *a* female, united by propinquity; family considerations; commercial interests; class association; or what not.

Affinities at least have the grace to presuppose a special sex-attraction. They argue for the ultimate goal of special and permanent selection, even if they fail to reach it.

That there will be many failures during the journey from the sense-conscious life, to the soul-conscious life, is a foregone conclusion. The pathway of Love has always been a thorny one, but those who are on the high ground may look across into the rose-strewn garden, and know that the little god is aiming his arrows at the interior nature of those whom he would unite. He is not blind. His sight is illumined and he sees that the soul can unite only with its mate. True it is that "the course of true love never did run smooth," but let us hope that the time is coming when it will be less thorny.

There are no mismates in soul-union.

This truth is the "secret of secrets" of the Hermetics. It is the hidden wisdom of the initiates; the alchemical mysteries of the Ancients. It is told to us in the fairy story of the Sleeping Princess—a story which is found in the folk-lore of every country of the globe. It is the philosopher's stone, which when found, opens the door to all wisdoms.

There can be no mismates in soul-union.

Neither can there be any sexual "temptation," or desire outside of this union, when once found.

"But never shall he faint or fall

Who lists to hear, o'er every fate,

The sweeter and the higher call

    Of his true mate.

I hear it wheresoe'er I rove;

She holds me safe from shame or sin;

The holy temple of her love

    I worship in."

A time when "the twain shall be" virtually, "one flesh" and the "outside as the inside" is not a chimerical dream.

When the physical body is as much reverenced as is the spiritual; when in fact, the soul is revealed (unveiled) to our mortal consciousness; when the mind has been freed from its load of prejudices and fears and doubts and belief in sin; then we shall, indeed, truly see each other.

We do not see each other now, unless perhaps we have developed that spiritual insight which is not blinded by appearances, but which contacts the interior nature. But the revealing, the uncovering process has begun. We have come to the time so long anticipated; so earnestly promised, when "naked and unashamed" we should "re-enter the lost Paradise."

Well, the women, God bless them, are as naked as the tender morality of our police officials will permit and as unashamed as it is possible to be with the handicap of a puritanical ancestry, which was so evil-minded as to suspect God himself of sin when He formed the "wicked" body.

Prudists may howl; and legislators may legislate; but the course of the Cosmic Law which would free us and bestow upon us Peace and Love and Happiness without stint, has never been stopped, although it has been obstructed.

Let us examine some points of the Hidden Wisdom, in the light of this postulate, and see if the conclusion is not warranted.

CHAPTER VIII

THE HIDDEN WISDOM REVEALED

As we have previously observed, there is what may be termed a religious mysticism and a scientific mysticism. When viewed from the standpoint of the unprejudiced seeker, who finds the truth that is in everything, these two phases of mysticism are but photographs of the same subject taken from different points of view. So, too, mysticism itself is, in the final analysis, nothing more than a long-distance view of science.

Like the proverbial pot and kettle, which we are told made much noise over calling each other black, we find the scientist frequently disdains the mystic, and the mystic may retaliate with equal disapproval of the scientist's position. Both are right, each from his point of view. Each is looking at life from an opposite end of the same pole. The scientist looks at the effect and the mystic at the cause. In their final calculations they arrive at the same conclusion, although they call it by different names.

The scientist says that everything proceeds from the one eternal energy. The mystic perceives the spiritual co-existent with the external. Religious mysticism calls it "God's word made manifest." In reference to this definition of religious mysticism, perhaps the phraseology used by William Ralph Inge, in his "Christian Mysticism," is the best possible exposition of the position of the religious mystic, if we may separate the two phases. Inge says: "Religious mysticism may be defined as the attempt to realize the presence of the living God in the soul and in nature, or more generally as the attempt to realize in thought and in feeling the imminence of the temporal in the eternal, and the eternal in the temporal."

Which is to say exactly what the scientific mystic says, using other terminology; and likewise what the physicist says or will ultimately say, as his researches lead him into the finer and finer realms of discovery.

The scientific mystic, like Archimedes, believes that in order to measure the purpose of external creation, he must "base his fulcrum somewhere beyond."

The scientific mystic, therefore, starts from the center of the Circle; from the crux of creation; and he finds the X, which is the hypothetical base of algebraical science—the unknown quantity of which sex is the symbol. Reasoning from effect back to cause and from cause forward to effect the mystic finds the equation complete, perfect, and likewise simple; but it is simple only after we have deciphered it. Like the prize puzzles which are designed to exercise the inductive faculties, mysticism, when we have not the key, is a most tantalizing enigma. Most "practical" persons dismiss it with the same superficial idea that they entertain in regard to puzzles, saying "it is only a puzzle"—utterly ignoring the value of exercising the inductive reasoning faculties.

Fairy stories are popularly supposed to be for the entertainment and amusement of children. In reality they are the universal language of symbolism. There is not a single fairy story which has not been handed down from generation to generation, and, what is more suggestive, each story is told with astonishing lack of variation, in every tongue and throughout every nation on this earth.

The stories involving the turning of men into animals and their final restoration to human form, as a reward for some service, some sacrifice, typifies the two-fold nature of Man. He may live in his animal, or exterior nature; or he may develop his spiritual, or interior nature; through service; through unselfish love. Our limited mortal consciousness is responsible for the tendency to personify everything, instead of to realize the principles underlying all expression. God and the Devil have been the personification of the two phases of the principles of Evolution, from animal man to spiritual man.

Romulus and Remus have been presented as an actual and specific instance of twins; likewise Castor and Pollux. Almost every child instinctively alludes to himself or herself, as either "the good little me" or the "bad little me." "O, I didn't do that; it was the bad little Dorothy," or "Harold," as the case may be, is the child-like way of expressing the innate consciousness that there is an interior and an exterior nature to all of us.

The union of gods with mortals, which forms the gist of Mythological tales, symbolizes the god-like and the mortal qualities inherent in human nature. Mortals raised to the abode of the gods; and the gods descended into mortal life; symbolize the interchangeability of what we term matter and spirit—the power of transmutation of the lower into the higher life.

Volumes could be written upon the subject, and we will therefore try to confine our reviews to the symbolical traditions which deal most directly with the relations of the sexes.

In religious symbology, the story of the ark stands as the supreme type of creation, through the conjunction of the sexes. _

The cherubim are, when all is said and done, nothing more, nor yet less, than spiritual children—the result of spiritual sex-union.

And in this later synoptic mysticism of the ark of the Covenant, we are informed that "every gift within the tabernacle is willingly offered." If we will but contemplate the volumes of wisdom contained within that sentence, we cannot fail to conclude that every infinitesimal particle of coercion in whatsoever shape and form, individual, economic, ethical, or religious, must be excluded from the regenerated, perfect, ideal sex-relation; otherwise we do not attain it.

If the Ancients seemed to take some of these folk-lore stories too literally, we of this "practical" age, do not take them literally enough.

We have imagined that sex, and the sex function, began and ended in the physical. This view is excusable in the case of the materialist, if there really be such a person but it is obviously a stupid view for the theologian, who regards this life as the door to spiritual life. Since sex is the cause and the result of what we know of creation; since it is the foundation of all the qualities that we know as spiritual laws; friendship; unselfishness; fidelity; paternal solicitude—it is absolutely certain that the most beautiful things we know here must have a correspondence in the life hereafter. Of these beautiful things in life, babies come first; with birds and flowers and music as fitting accessories.

But to return to the ark of the covenant. The perpetual flame on the altar (the center) is the undying Flame of spiritual love—and by that we mean sex-love, let it be understood. If we seem to repeat this too frequently it is because of the almost general habit of the race to apologize for sex-love. The erroneous idea obtains, that spiritual love is sexless. All too frequently we come across the phrase, "with a love that has in it nothing of human love," the writer evidently anxious to convey the impression of tremendous spirituality and the consequent elimination of the sex function.

And so we emphasize once more, and we may do so again, the assurance that the symbol of the never-dying flame upon the altar is typical of the never-dying spirit of sex-love. Spirit is ever symbolized by flame, as in the "flaming sword" of the archangel.

The Deity upon the seat of the altar symbolizes the bi-une Sex-principle of creation.

The reason that the Jewish people have claimed that they were "God's chosen people" is because, in their symbolism of the ark of the Covenant, all Israel was grouped under the tabernacle. The formation of the tabernacle proves that it typifies the mother's womb. The tabernacle was guarded by the priests who *were sworn to purity*; thus they symbolized the esoteric truth that the pure spiritual sex-union bestows immortal god-hood.

Let us take another story, that of the life-token. This is best told in the story of the Holy Grail, although it is found in all the fairy-books of all nations, in the language and form befitting the race to which it belongs.

In the original, that is in the earliest recitals of this life-token story, we find that the thing left behind, as a *center* (which is always guarded and protected in various ways), was a tree. Here, we have the phallic symbol as the life-token. But in the story of the Holy Grail, the cup is the life token to be guarded; it is the sacred symbol of the quest and it is of a design resembling the red rose of the Templars. This time it is the yoni—literally the *chalice* of the *holy communion*; the centre of the radiant circle, which is the answer to all the problems within the radius. It is the search for, and the finding of, the balance in counterpartal union. It is the X of Being, and only the purest and the noblest of the Knights of the "Round Table" essay the difficult quest. The "mound of Venus" is another name for the "Round Table."

Again is emphasized the necessity for purity, and this purity, although including all the spiritual qualities: fidelity; bravery; self-sacrifice; humanity; love of truth; culminates in sexual purity.

"Blessed are the pure in heart (the pulse of the soul) for they shall see God." We revise this latter part, and we say "for they shall be *gods*."

Let us consider the story of the "sleeping Princess." She is depicted as a princess, first of all, because she is the daughter of a king; a king is an earthly ruler, or exalted person. Esoterically, she is the daughter of the exalted God, and she is the soul. Sometimes this story is told in the male gender, but everywhere the essential points are the same.

Wagner, who is known as a Mystic, has illustrated the story in Brunhilde and Siegfried. Brunhilde is an immortal—a goddess, who renounces her immortality to become a woman.

She sleeps on the top of a high mountain and she is surrounded by a circle of flame; and here she sleeps, despite all efforts to arouse her, until awakened by the touch of Siegfried—the one human being in all the universe who could awaken the sleeping princess.

The high mountain symbolizes the highest love of which we are capable. To reach the soul of the exalted woman, typified in the fairy-story by the word princess, and later, by Wagner, as the goddess, man must be her mate. *No other can enter the womb of her soul*, though many may effect an entrance to the outer court.

This truth, as absolute as life itself, solves all the problems of the mystery of love and its joys and sorrows. No soul can wholly, unreservedly love the "wrong" one. Though we may love and die of the pain of unrequited loving, yet love is its own self-justification, and its own reward. The pathway of love leads up the mountain top, but no one who reaches the summit shall fail to find that for which he seeks.

The soul of man, and of woman, has been playing a game of blind-man's bluff—a fitting name for the game it is, too. Unable to see anything but the exterior nature, and longing for success in the search, we have frantically grabbed here and there, and appropriated that which we grabbed, with a self complacency and an egotism of which little Jack Horner would be ashamed.

In the symbolical rites and ceremonies of secret orders, such as the Ancient Alchemists; the Hermetics; the Rosicrusians; and in modern times, the Free Masons, we have this story of the search for the ultimate balance of soul union, told in language veiled unless we are fit to know; but openly enough if we are fit. And in all these orders (alleged guardians of the hidden wisdom) we have varying degrees of initiation; and in each degree the initiate must undergo certain trials to prove his fearlessness; his fidelity; his fitness, in other words, for the final revealment of all, which is the initiation into the "holy of holies;" the "secret chamber" and the degree of "mastership."

In the order of Masonry, the highest degree is that of the Templar. The symbol of the Templars is the red rose on the cross, together with the star and the crescent. The star preserves the esotericism of its nomenclature, in whatever sphere it is used, namely, the power of radiating light. It stands for the radiant center. The Knights Templar sought the radiant center to complete their half circle, and when they should have found, they were to become radiant with the light of spiritual power. That they originally at least, understood the way of this initiation, is evident by the symbol of the rose and the cross—the combined phallus and yoni.

This fact is the underlying cause of the open and hereditary enmity of the Church of Rome for the modern order of Freemasons. The Church sought to specialize in the persons of the Virgin Mary and her Son the eternal principles of the "way of the cross." The temporal power of the Church could be built up only by offering a complete system of salvation within the church itself. At the same time, the utter degradation of Sex, which had reached its depths under Roman civilization, called for as complete a reversion of the ideas of the Ancient sex-worshippers, as was consistent with the truth.

Hence we find the extreme attitude of the Church opposing all reference to sex as other than a part of the temptations of the Evil One, although they did retain the central truth typified by the Holy Virgin Mother, and the pure and perfect child.

The Alchemists are supposed to have been imbued with the desire and, to some extent, at least, were regarded as having the knowledge of how to make gold. This gold-making was always accomplished by transmutation of the baser (lower) metals; also, the knowledge of how to accomplish this transmutation was possible only to one possessing "the philosopher's stone."

If we will but remember that this "philosopher's stone" was of such a purity that it was almost impossible to find it; that, although several initiates claimed to possess the stone, yet no visible proof of its existence, or of gold resulting from lead or copper, was ever offered; and again if we will realize the fine distinction between the words "found" and "discovered," and take note that the word "found" is used almost invariably in connection with those who claimed to possess the stone, we will arrive at the obvious conclusion that the secret of the Alchemists was of an interior nature. We "discover" outside of ourselves; we "find" within. Above all, the "stone of great purity" is the same that was raised at Babylon, supplanting the yoni, which is to say, the phallic symbol.

A philosopher is one who is wise in his interior nature; his wisdom is of the esoteric quality; we do not apply the term "philosopher" to either great educators, or great financiers; but to those whose activities are turned within.

The force which is manifested in the lower desires and passions, when transmuted into spiritual channels, opens the door to the golden light of illumination.

To become in reality a Prince of the Rosy Cross bestows the exaltation and the power, typified by that of an earthly prince—one who is exalted above the common man.

It is doubtful, indeed, if many of the ancient alchemists attained to this exalted degree in its true significance; and we may readily believe that in an age in which wealth was so eagerly sought; temporal power so much desired; where deception was almost general; that few lived the requisite purity of life to have accomplished the transmutation; so today there is not one in a thousand of the many who have taken the degree of "Knight Templar," who recognizes its esoteric meaning.

But words have a trick of trapping us, and we note that the word "taken" is invariably used in referring to modern Masonic initiation. Verily they have "taken" the degree in its outward semblance. They have not attained to its powers and privileges.

Nor can they do so, when they exclude the very "gate of life" from the order. They may become masons (builders of the temple), but how can they become Architects, when they have not entered the tabernacle?

In a search for hidden meanings, and for a secret tradition which is believed to be discoverable in Kabalistic and Hermetic literature, we find, if we possess true insight, the one indubitable truth, subordinating all the other symbols, namely that of the supremacy, the finality, of the sublimated sex-union, resulting in immortal mastership.

Most modern interpreters of the archives of these ancient philosophers ignore the sexual significance of the arcana, but a glimpse at the symbols will readily convince the initiated of their identity with sexual symbology.

For example in "The History of Transcendental Magic," by Eliphas Levi (Abbe Constant), translated by Arthur Edward Waite, there is a plate used to illustrate the author's theory of Alchemy, which he concludes "had two aspects, one a physical and the other a moral one." The sexual, as well as the spiritual, significance is ignored, but this may be due to a disinclination to reveal the secret meaning of the alchemical symbols, or it may be due to a materialistic tendency on the part of the compiler.

The plates, however, speak for themselves, and in one, ascribed to Basil-Valentine, an alchemist of the Fifteenth century, called "The Great Hermetic Arcanum," the supreme and significant point of the illustration, shows, within the circle of Experience, through which the initiate travels in his search for the supreme god-head, two doves, holding in their beaks a crown. The doves are perfectly matched. The crown is balanced between them, and the figure tops the circle, under the heading "regeneration."

In another plate, which the author presents as "the Philosophic Cross, or Plan of the Third Temple as prophesied by Ezekiel," we note again, that the crown of the symbolical temple represents the red rose upon a cross, within a radiant circle; beneath this is a mother-eagle with outstretched wings, shielding her little brood, and on either side a tree and a flowering rosebush.

Here is the symbol par excellence of generation. The creative function of the male and the female in procreative conjunctivity.

The employment of the eagle as a religious symbol may be traced back to the civilization of the Hittites.

Only a few years ago, two English archæologists discovered a double-headed eagle in Asia. This was identical with those seen perpetuating religious rites and ceremonies of the sex-worshipers. An eagle holding in its talons a serpent is an emblem well known today. The origin of the adoption of the eagle as a religious, though not necessarily a "sacred," symbol by prehistoric races, may easily be imagined, if we consider that the eagle is a bird of tremendous power; and that it soars to unreachable heights; and that it unquestionably was at some time seen to swoop down and carry off the serpent, possibly even during their ceremonies of serpent-worship.

This idea becomes quite convincing when we also remember that the ceremonies of the serpent worshipers were carried on, as far as feasible, upon the mountain. We allude to this stage of religious history as "serpent worship," but when we realize the points of analogy between the serpent and the phallus it is apparent that the serpent was only the nature-emblem of generation, as manifested by the male principle.

"The eagle and the dove" is a phrase employed today to illustrate the law of antithesis, and it is more than probable that the eagle represented the lower nature of the sex-relation, in juxtaposition to the higher, as the dove is emblematical of the spiritualized aspect of sex-love. We have an analogy to that of the eagle and the dove in the Biblical allusion to "the last day; when God will separate the 'sheep from the goats,'" Here again is a pertinent reference to the sex nature. The goat is a symbol of sensuality and lust, principally because he has perverted sexual proclivities, notably that of coercion. For this reason, Classical Mythology employs the satyr, a creature half man and half goat, to typify the lowest form of the sex call in man.

On the other hand, the lamb is the type of gentleness and affection, and although in outward appearance the lamb and the goat are not dissimilar, their natures are antithetical.

In estimating the God-idea of the Ancients, many mistakes have arisen by confounding religious symbols with the "sacred" symbols. The race-mind was in its kindergarten stage, and all ideals were instilled by means of pictures—a method which even the present hour finds most effective.

In modern theological symbolism we have God and the Devil; Heaven and Hell; angels and demons, to illustrate by antithesis.

They all belong to religious symbology, but only those which teach spiritual ideals are denominated "sacred."

"Riding the goat," alleged to be the almost invariable initiatory prelude to fitness for membership in all secret orders, means, first of all, that the would-be initiate must have control over his lower sexual desires. If he cannot control the goat instincts within his nature, he stands small chance of taking the higher degrees of spiritual regeneration, through transmutation.

In another symbolic chart presenting the secrets of alchemical transmutation, we find depicted "The Gate of Eternal Wisdom," and we are further informed that this "gate" also brings "knowledge of God." The design of this cave-like aperture should betray its esoteric meaning. It is situated under a mound, upon which trees are planted. The inscriptions on the corrugated walls of the cave, are evidently designed to resemble seven lotus petals, and are set forth as the seven mysteries. Inscriptions warning against profanation of this sacred gate, and also promising eternal life and glory to the true initiate, inspire the intrepid and deter the doubtful. Of these latter, several are outside the entrance. Two are on the steps leading to the mouth of the cave but their attitude bespeaks doubt of their worthiness. Only one has penetrated to the radiant center of the aperture, and there is room for but the one to enter the radiance of the solar gate, which truly bestows a knowledge that is "of God."

Sex Symbology is a subject that calls for a large volume devoted to this special side of it, and we cannot hope to do more here than to touch a few of the almost universal proofs of the contention which is the purpose of this book, namely, that the supreme goal of life, typified in every religion, every philosophy, and in the intuitional knowledge of the human mind, is spiritual sex-union; and that this can be accomplished only by counterparts; the two halves of the bi-une god seed uniting in one immortal and complete pair—a man and a woman. Not, we must again emphasize, not in a hermaphroditic personality, but in two perfect complementaries—mates; not *one* but *a pair*.

In another exposition of Hermetic secrets we discover the amazing statement that "the alchemist is found working throughout, in conjunction with a woman of the art; *they begin and they attain together*."

This should be plain enough. Small chance, indeed, either would have of attaining alone. But if this suggestion is not sufficient (and either from design or from failure to comprehend the significance of it, the translator seems to have missed the point), we are introduced to a symbolical figure-study, which shows a Chalice in which the sun and the moon are personified (the solar-man and the solar-woman), with the god Vulcan (fire) seated between them. Underneath this "twain-one" symbol a mortal man and a mortal woman are kneeling on either side of a cone-shaped and dome-tipped furnace, which is lighted by a feeble candle. But their attitude of prayer bespeaks the hope that this earthly flame will be transmuted by their prayers and aspirations; by their reverential attitude toward the divine character of the function of mating, into the immortal and unquenchable flame typified by the god of fire himself.

In another series of symbolical plates, purporting to be the story of Metallic transmutation, but representing, above all, the story of manifestation from the Divine to the human and again to the spiritualized and perfected Adam and Eve—(the solar man and the solar woman), we again see that from generation to regeneration the work is accomplished by man and woman in conjunction.

These plates bear the hall-marks of Christian appropriation of Hermetic symbolism, as peculiarly applicable to the Church, but the central doctrine of salvation through sex-regeneration, is retained. Whether consciously or not, is a question.

Modern commentators and translators of alchemical literature insist that such documents are palpably related to the secret, or secrets, of metallic transmutation. That they prove the search for, if not the existence of, a "magic solvent" that resolves the baser metals into gold; but, as far as known, such a compound has not yet been discovered or, if it ever was, it has since been lost and evades all attempts at rediscovery. But if we read these alchemical treatises as they relate to transmutation of sex-love from the pro-creative function to regeneration through spiritual or counterpartal union (solar mates), we have the key to every statement.

A writer tells of an instance which is recorded among alchemical archives, where "an unknown master testified to his possession of the mystery" (supposedly of metallic transmutation), but it is added that "he had not proceeded to the work because he had failed to meet an *elect woman*, who was necessary thereto." In other words, applying this statement in its obviously logical sense, the unknown master knew the esoteric meaning of the alchemical postulate, but not having met his female complement, he could not testify to the results of this transmutation. An "elect woman" would hardly be necessary in the work of metallic transmutation.

Small wonder that the "alchemist" abandoned the work of turning lead and copper into gold. If he had found the key of keys, he cared little whether lead were lead, or whether gold remained gold, or melted into thin air. The golden light of illumination showed him all things in their purpose, and gold as a metal meant no more to him than did the so-called "baser" metals.

Commenting upon this statement, the translator observes: "Those Hermetic texts which bear a spiritual interpretation and are as if a record of spiritual experience, present, like the literature of physical alchemy, the following aspects of symbolism: the marriage of sun and moon; of a mystical king and queen; a union between natures which are *one* at the *root*, but diverse in manifestation; a transmutation which follows this union and an abiding glory therein."

If we will remember that the solar-man was personified by the Ancients as the sun; and the solar-woman by the moon, we have the first and salient points of the original Hermetic secrets, however much they may have degenerated from their spiritual to their physical application. The probabilities are that owing to the disapproval of the Christian Hierarchy, only the most veiled terminology was permissible. This view is more logical than is the one that the esoteric meaning was lost sight of.

The marriage of an hypothetical or "mystical king and queen" bespeaks exaltation of the two conjoining persons, male and female, but this exaltation is in consciousness, and not in mere personality. The terms "king" and "queen" are nothing more or less than symbols of an exalted (spiritualized) state.

And, in passing, we may here mention the fact that the language of lovers testifies to this intuitional realization. "My queen!" exclaims the enraptured lover, although in social station his beloved one may be only a scullery maid; and certainly, neither the beauty nor the goodness nor the wisdom of earthly kings and queens would be sufficient to inspire the comparison.

It is ever the soul calling for the mate who, when found, will exalt the "twain-one" into the immortal powers and immortal wealth imperfectly symbolized by earthly rulers, making "right royal queens and kings of common clay."

The third aspect of the symbolism tells of "an union between two natures which are one at the root, but diverse in manifestation." And the alchemist who sought the physical interpretation of this, promised that, as earth, air, and fire and water were the elements "out of which all manifestation is composed," it only remained for someone to discover the exact proportion of each of these elementary substances in a specific compound; this accomplished, copper for example, could be dissolved into its constituent parts and re-solved again in the proportions which formed gold, a thing which we are not prepared to say could not be accomplished, but a thing which we do say, would not even be attempted by one who had found the secret of the interior transmutation, because having attained to the radiant center, he would realize the "glory of the worlds," and gold, as metal, would be to him of far less value than the emerald of the grass; the pearls of dew upon the rose; the scent of the lotus; the song of birds; the laughter of children.

How vain and foolish to imagine that a philosopher would think it worth while to search for gold, as a metal. He would not even consider the ambition worthy the parchment used to preserve the record of his labors.

But to find the golden light from the radiant center of pure and unquenchable love—that were indeed worthy of ages of research. For are we not promised, the "glory of the world" if we will seek and find? And he who truly seeks will absolutely find. What is the glory of the world? Is it fame, or wealth, or lands, or gems or kingdoms?

Love is the only glory worthy of the name.

"For Life with all its yield of joy and woe

And hope and fear—believe the aged friend—

Is just our chance at the prize o' learning love."

When we realize the esoteric meaning of this aspect of the ancient alchemical symbol, namely, that the two halves of the one whole, manifesting diversely as male and female, are reunited, we come to the fourth aspect of the symbol mentioned, and the "transmutation which follows this union and the abiding glory therein," is the inevitable and logical sequential answer.

An *abiding* glory must be founded upon spiritual substantiability. Transmutation is not synonymous with, extinction, or elimination, or abandonment. We *transmute* the lower into the higher, the exterior into the interior, the physical into the spiritual. This is the sum and substance of the "Ancient Wisdom."

There is no eccentric change or transition from one phase or plane of life, into another. It is neither logical nor justifiable to assume that Sex is limited to the physical, or the astral or the psychic, or any other specific planes of consciousness. These planes are not distinctively separable anyway. They are merely *names* which we use to distinguish degrees, or limitations of consciousness.

The statement that the "two halves are reunited" is almost invariably misinterpreted to imply an annihilation, or absorption of individuality, into some sort of vaporous, formless, sexless Thing; but why this should be so misconstrued is a puzzle, any more than that bringing together the two halves of an orange which had been divided, would result in the destruction of that edible; or any more than bringing together a glove fitting the right hand and its mate fitting the left hand, would destroy the shape and usefulness of this article. The comparison may be a homely one, but it is understandable.

It takes two to make a pair. Mistake it not, and further, there is no *abiding glory* in this world or in the next or in any other sphere, that is not founded upon the deep, intense and eternal love of man and woman.

CHAPTER IX

WHAT CONSTITUTES SEX IMMORALITY?

The average mind, nurtured in apprehensive awe of that race fetish called Public Opinion, is inordinately afraid of words.

"Atheist," "infidel," "ungodly" are epithets which have been used as mental clubs, with temporary effect, to beat back the wave of religious and scientific Rationalism, which punctuated the last century.

These words have now lost much of their terror, even to the undeveloped consciousness of the average, because it has been shown that the God-idea which rational thought fain would substitute for the old revengeful Deity, has not annihilated the world, but quite to the contrary has resulted in a happier and higher ideal of godhood than that which the early Church postulated.

Epithets are the mental bulwarks of the powers of resistance against Evolution.

Ignorance is fearful of the unknown, and the knights of Enlightenment have ever had to fight their way through the ranks of abuse and criticism and misrepresentation.

Free-love is a phrase with which even the most intrepid advocate of rational thought hesitates to claim affiliation; and yet the goal of our highest endeavors must be a state of Society where Love, the god, is free from the mire of corruption, and the bonds of slavery.

Let us not be afraid of so harmless a thing as a word, remembering the case of the little girl who ran to her mother crying with indignation because someone had alluded to her as an "aristocrat." She did not know what the word meant, and so resented it as something undeserved.

When we examine into what the phrase free-love really means, we will not be so fearful of its sound.

To whom is this epithet most frequently applied?

Is it to the average man who is known to be a Lothario in matters of sex? Not at all. He is referred to as a "gay bachelor" or as one who is "sowing his wild oats" or some other phrase, which in no way affects his social standing.

Is it applied to women of the half-world, to recognized, and legalized prostitution? Never! It is significant of the real meaning of free-love that the term is never used in connection with what modern reform has aptly designated the "white slave" traffic, for the obvious reason that nowhere is Love so un-free; so enslaved and bound and murdered as in this phase of woman's degradation.

Nor is the term applied to unfaithful wives, because in this type of defiance of traditional sex-ethics there is always the spirit of self-accusation; a tacit, if not open, admission of wrong-doing.

We never hear the awful accusation of "free-lover" hurled at the young woman who has, what the world calls, "sinned," because, forsooth, she pays the price of her deviation from social standards (when discovered) by ostracism, and not infrequently by a broken heart, or by sinking further into the depths of bondage; and so here again it is evident that there is no freedom for whatever spirit of love actuates her conduct.

It must be admitted that the term "free-love" is applied only to those who openly claim the right to bestow their affections and indulge in the sex-relationship, independent of the marriage ceremony. It matters not whether this claim includes but one mate, or several. It is the demand that they shall not forfeit their right to respect and morality, which is resented by the many who still conform to traditional customs, and which general conformity results in investing the term "free-love" with an unpleasant odor.

Public opinion puts a premium upon deceit.

Such intimate matters as marriage and divorce are really no concern of any person other than the contracting or the "distracted" parties.

The public is too concerned with trivialities and too little with Truth. Nothing short of national insanity permits the existence of divorce-courts, and the necessity for married persons desiring to live apart, to slander and abuse each other like pickpockets before they may act upon such a decision.

Some time ago the public press was filled with the minutest details of the love story of a woman, who had lived for fifteen years hidden from the world because she loved a man well enough to pay that price.

She might have insisted that the man obtain a divorce from his wife, to whom he had been married seventeen or more years, and thus win the approval of society. But this woman placed love above all material things, and she preferred to take nothing from the wife. The love of her husband the wife did not possess and, it would seem, did not care for particularly. When through the accident of the man's death the story came to light, the press was flooded with letters from prominent club-women and from clergymen and others, stating upon what terms, if any, this love-recluse should be forgiven.

Most of them decided that she should not be forgiven; a few seemed to think that if she "repented" and lived thereafter a "pure" life, she might in time be worthy of their forgiveness.

Such a spectacle! America will yet share the reputation with England of being a nation without a sense of humor.

Eagerly the representative members of society "rush in where angels fear to tread" upon any and all occasions to air their opinions upon other people's conduct and thus prove their own virtue.

The fact that this woman was not in any position to be forgiven or unforgiven; that she was sublimely unconscious of and wholly indifferent to their opinions; that she was unaware of any necessity for either shame or repentance; seems not to have entered the silly brains of these keepers of the public morals. She had loved one man with a fidelity, a whole-heartedness, and a loftiness of self-sacrifice which are as rare as they are great in these days of pretense and hypocritical virtue, and she had paid the full price for her idealism. She did not repine or regret. She only suffered, not alone because of her unenviable notoriety, but because Death had taken her loved one from her. Surely this was indeed an evidence of real love in an unreal civilization, which should have brought out the fearless sympathy and approval of every good woman in the land. It should have been food for sermons in every pulpit in Christendom, that a modern woman preferred solitary confinement with the man she loved to the usual method of procedure, which insists upon the respectable position of wife, no matter at what cost to another.

But this is Society's estimate of Love and Truth and Virtue, and it is small wonder if real people become indifferent to Society's feelings.

If the term free-love were really synonymous with sex-promiscuity, we would hear it used in connection with those whose frequent divorces are the subject of press comment, but we do not, because by their outward concession to established ethics they subscribe to the demands of Convention.

The term, in its opprobrious sense, is almost always applied to women, because for many centuries the men have claimed their right to personal liberty in matters connected with the sex-relation, and until women of the self-respecting and educated class began to openly emulate the example of the male, there was no occasion to use the phrase. Men come under its lash only when they, too, concede to women the right to respectability notwithstanding defiance of tradition.

All of which goes to prove that the public mind is in reality sufficiently clear on the matter of distinction between sex promiscuity and free-love. It is likewise obvious that the opprobrium that attaches to the phrase is not aimed at promiscuity but at the claim to personal liberty in matters of the sex-relation and defiance of Public Opinion which demands either ostensible concurrence in its standards, or punishment for openly transgressing them.

The result of this unjust (and unfit, in the light of our other advanced ideas) attitude toward the most important function of life, has resulted in one of two lines of conduct as woman's only free choice.

Either she must resort to deception, hypocrisy and pretense, shielding her secret excursions into forbidden paths, by feigning a scorn and abhorrence for the doctrine of free-love, the while she secretly indulges her sex-nature, more or less promiscuously, or else she is forced to repress all her natural instincts, and not infrequently these instincts are abnormally strong because of pre-natal and inherited influences.

Both of these courses, the only two which are open to the average woman, are disastrous to the sex, and through them to the race, because women are the mothers of men, and any course which binds and fetters the free spirit of woman hampers race-improvement.

Repression of the natural functions of her being results in physical disease, and ultimately in mental weakness. Unnatural expression of the sex-function, under the ban of compulsion, whether through the compulsion of marriage or through the more flagrant type of commercial prostitution, is death to the best development of the race.

Women, through the urge of economic necessity, or through the religious ideal of wifely submission and fidelity to their "Lord and Master" have been compelled to develop a craftiness and an artificial "modesty" which, in most cases, passes for femininity, and deceives, as it is intended to do, the average man.

For centuries, a woman's only profession was matrimony. Her education for this profession consisted first of all of complete ignorance of all that relates to the most intimate and most vital part of her nature—the function of sex. In the occasional instances where she had inherited a degree of mentality which could not be dwarfed, she must at least feign ignorance; and so, while secretly aware of every emotion of the male, and covertly playing upon his sex-nature in her task of "catching a husband," it is small wonder that women have developed the traits of the cat animal, and are frequently both treacherous and cruel.

Indeed, it is only because the Female Principle is the attracting and conserving power of the bi-une sex-love, that she has broken through these mental fetters, and in a few rare instances has hurled defiance at the devils of convention and tradition and claims justification of her own sex-nature, and her right to her own person, despite the epithet of "free-love."

Woman's partial emancipation in some instances has, no doubt, "gone to her head," as it were, and we see many women confounding license with liberty;

mistaking passion for Love; and exchanging restraint for debauchery.

The average woman is either almost entirely lacking in sex desire or she is abnormally active in that function. In truth, the same state of affairs prevails here, as in so many other phases of our modern life, namely, there is no balance. We are a civilization of extremes; we are one-sided, abnormal; distorted. We are seeking the pivotal point of our destiny, which is the soul, but few have reached that point. Those who have not, are groping through the jungles of the mental plane of consciousness, upheld on the one hand by the upward trend of their being, which seeks the level of the soul-conscious state; and held back on the other hand by the trammels of the sense-conscious type from which the race has developed to its present condition.

Those instances where women indulge in excesses are comparatively rare in proportion to numbers, and they loom large in perspective because of their very incongruity with our ideals of womanly conduct. The vast majority of women may be safely trusted to use their sex-freedom, when it shall have truly arrived, for the purpose of finding that one and only mate which their souls instinctively know to be our rightful heritage—the proverbial "pearl of great price" which insures immortality in the bliss of union with our Beloved.

Love, when freed from the illusions of sense; from the shackles of commercialism; from the bonds of error regarding the meaning and purpose of marriage; freed from selfishness and licentiousness; will solve the question of sex-promiscuity. This for the obvious reason that Love seeks its own. If left free to seek, it will find.

But, if sex promiscuity is far from being free-love, if the doctrine of sex freedom is fraught with many dangers under our present social system, it must be conceded that no one method of social evolution, thus far devised, can be recommended as ideally perfect. The best that we can hope to do is to emphasize the importance and the sacredness and the innate purity of the sex-relation, while conceding to both sexes all the personal liberty possible.

And above all, we should avoid condemnation of those who claim the right to freedom, lest we cover up a condition which can but be the better for being open to the light. Particularly should we shield women from the charge of immorality, and licentiousness, when we see them straying down the by-paths of the senses, in their quest for freedom, remembering that the centuries of repression and submission and consequent deception have left their mark upon woman's temperament.

Man has for ages boasted of his sex virility; of his conquests in what he has termed "love." Not infrequently a man's choice of a wife is the result of much seeking in the garden of Life; and much sipping of the honey from the various flowers that grow therein. Often, indeed, a man frankly tells the woman he would marry that he knows he loves her above all other women for the convincing reason that he has tried so many and none have held him. Should a woman make the same confession and draw the same conclusion, he would be horrified.

It must be admitted, then, that the term "free-lovers" is applied only to those who defy Public Opinion and claim their right to respect and morality despite their defiance of Society's false standards of morality. These standards are false because they are based upon criticism and censure of results instead of upon motives.

Society ignores, if it does not actually encourage, frivolous flirtations, and frowns most harshly upon instances of real love. It sets the seal of disapproval and ostracism upon those who, because of circumstances or possibly because of indifference to man-made laws, take their affairs into their own hands and refuse to exhibit either penitence or shame when the world discovers that they neglected the marriage ceremony. If two persons truly love each other and there is nothing to interfere with their undergoing the publicity of a marriage ceremony, well and good, unless, indeed, it is a matter of principle with them that our social customs are a fetich. But there are innumerable instances where there are obstacles to unions which to overcome would involve hardships and suffering to others, or where absurd laws prevent marriage, and where two persons loving each other, prefer to pay the price of social ostracism to separation. Such as these lose nothing by Society's disapproval, but Society does lose something by persecuting those who are independent enough and honest enough to act from motive, rather than from custom, and who insist upon maintaining their self-respect, in the face of criticism. Self-respect is not related to braggadocio.

It must be admitted that as yet there are few persons who have the courage to endure martyrdom for their convictions, which is, perhaps, just as well, because the majority are unable to distinguish between brazen shamelessness and unashamedness. The average woman will stick to the safe habit of dissembling.

Women have learned the lesson of the cat too thoroughly to jump immediately from the back-yard of Deception to the front porch of Truth.

In this one respect at least, however much she may indulge her desire for frankness in other directions, a woman will lie valiantly, self-protectingly, and continually, even though she follow in secret the example of the cat, which (seeing its master come home from the hunt with a string of birds, and displaying, with much pride and satisfaction, the results of his prowess), conceived the idea that it would also be a fine thing for her to go forth and kill the canary. But to tabby's surprise, her ability was rewarded with chastisement; whereupon she pondered the question over and over: "How can it be, that what is virtue in man is vice in a cat?"

We are not told in the story what conclusion she arrived at, but we can imagine that her conclusion was that which women have arrived at, in a similar situation, to wit: man is unjust and unreasonable, but he is also stronger than I am, and therefore, while I shall follow his example, I shall take good care to hide the feathers.

In the meantime, we are crossing the bridge that leads from the jungles of our animal nature, where prowl the beasts of deceit; greed; selfishness; sensuality; vanity; avarice; and domination; to the Heights, illumined by Love set free.

Let us not jostle and crowd each other too harshly, while we are en route.

But, of course, we are confronted with the pertinent query as to what, if any, absolute standard of morality there can be in matters of the sex relation. Freedom is so easily misconstrued into implying sex-promiscuity; and monogamy, the final survival of the various systems of marriage, has in its modern as well as in its ancient aspect so much of coercion; and coercion is cited as the insuperable obstacle to attainment of the supreme state of spiritual sex-union, that the would-be initiate becomes confused, and is lost in a maze of paradoxes.

Moral distinctions are too fine for the undeveloped man-animal, and that is the reason why man-made laws have been necessary. The objection to them is not in their original intention, but in their failure to die after they have become senile.

Moral standards are as unstable as the shifting sands of the sea.

"Our moral sentiments," say Letourneau, "are simply habits incarnate in our brain, or instincts artificially created; and thus an act reputed culpable at Paris, or at London, may be, and frequently is, held innocent at Calcutta or at Pekin."

And Emerson, the intellectual Seer, says: "There is a soul at the centre of nature and over the will of every man, so that none of us can wrong the universe."

It is a colossal piece of impudent presumption, when we come to think about it, for Man to ask the Supreme, Absolute, Infinite Power to forgive him. But, if we cannot wrong the universe, we can and we do wrong ourselves and each other as mortals.

That is the whole gist of the story. We are constantly wronging ourselves and each other and calling upon God to support us in our strife when God cannot know aught save the call of Love.

The growing, evolving race, has found it necessary to establish certain loosely defined codes of morals and of social ethics, in the same way that man has bridled the horse that he may control him; incidentally, we may observe that where this bridle formerly included "blinders," it now permits the horse to see whither he is going.

Perhaps a brief survey of the standards of sexual morality which have upheld (or down-held, just as we look at it) the human race until now, may be illuminating.

It has been disputed, if, under the matriarchal system of polygamy, the moral condition of the people was higher than under the patriarchal system, and probably no satisfactory conclusion can be reached upon this point, save and except that any condition, however primitive, which permitted to the female freedom of choice, must be better than that in which she is the object of coercion. This is evident, because the degree of coercion can never, under any circumstances, be as great with the male as with the female.

Therefore, matriarchal polygamy is comparatively more nearly moral than is patriarchal polygamy, and when all is said and done, historic morality is comparative.

But from the standpoint of modern idealism matriarchal polygamy seems to be a very low estimate of moral conduct; and from the standpoint of sexual idealism it is a low standard; a standard only a degree higher than that of patriarchal polygamy—a standard which is the lineal descendant of the ethics of the marriage-by-capture period of human evolution, and from which we are today by no means free, owing to economic, religious, and ethical conditions.

There is a tacit acknowledgement on the part of the unorganized brotherhood of the Enlightened, that laws are made for the guidance of the masses. Unbridled ignorance is a dangerous force; as dangerous as an unbridled horse, unless it be that the horse exhibits intelligence enough to know where it is headed for and how to avoid obstacles en route.

And even as the laws of a community are made for the intellectually undeveloped, so the commandments were compiled for the spiritual guidance of the uninitiated.

We trust that it will not shock the sensibilities of the "pious" when we affirm and maintain and insist that the ten commandments are not "from God" in the letter of the statements, as postulated by Theology. They bear all the earmarks of the ancient Hebrew race-mind, which placed a man's "neighbor's wife" in the same category with "his ox and his ass and his house" and his other property and possessions.

There is but one commandment of the Most High God, alias Eros, and that is so interwoven into the fabric of creation that we cannot break it if we would, although we may and do break ourselves in trying to live in defiance of its immutability.

"We cannot wrong the universe!"

Our moral standards, in so far as they relate to the sexes, are at present the logical descent of Hebrew adherence to phallic worship, engrafted into the Roman outgrowth of the God-idea. Both the Hebrew and the Roman customs maintained the inferiority and the consequent subjugation of woman, despite the fact that the Roman Church exalted the Virgin as a personality; but the postulate of the Church that Mary was so exalted by a miracle, which never could be repeated, killed any forlorn hope which might have lurked within the female breast regarding a possible emulation of her example. No other woman might do more than cringe and crawl and beg and whine; or cajole and wheedle and buy the Holy Mother's intercession, which intercession, even if successful, could at best but secure her an eternal job in the Heavenly hierarchy, where, sexless, companionless, mateless, anæmic, she could look all day at a male God whom she could never presume to reach.

Rather a lonesome outlook for eternity, and it is small wonder that woman got discouraged at the prospect. The miracle is rather that she endured it so long.

But the Roman system had at least one virtue. It instilled into the mortal mind of its people a sub-conscious realization of the ideal of monogamy; not an ideal monogamy by a long way, but a monogamic ideal. They are quite different; but inasmuch as it is an outward semblance of a more spiritual conception of marriage than that of polygamy, it is the highest ideal yet realized for the many, and does duty in our present day and age, as consistent with our superior civilization.

Monogamy at least pretends to be a marriage by mutual consent; and even in the pretense there is the germ of a hope; but it would be folly to deny that underneath this appearance of marriage by mutual consent we see the remnants of the traditional idea of the right by purchase, and therefore we have the jealousy that arises by virtue of our property rights.

The right by purchase assuredly underlies our present-day marriage system, although it is disguised as economic necessity; as a religious sacrament; and as a suitable or a brilliant "catch"—a type of marriage by capture which forms the ideal of our own upper-class women and which the housemaid copies in her limited way.

Viewed from the surface evidence, the average woman of today is, as Kipling says, far "more deadly than the male." She is more unscrupulous in her methods; more unreasonable in her demands; more devoid of sentiment or sympathy; more fickle in her desires and more nagging in her complaints. But, when all is said and done, we must admit that woman is only expressing her inheritance. When she becomes balanced, the sexes will meet on common ground.

Woman's demand for better physical environment; for more comfort, and more justice; presages, after all, a higher and a more satisfactory idea of the marriage relationship. Underneath this materialistic demand, there is the silent voice of the soul calling for a more ideal marriage relation. It is the materialistic expression of a spiritual urge and will in time rise to higher ground. It is a demand for a better state than that which our grandmothers enjoyed, or endured.

We have seen in the history of marriage, that the estimate of sexual immorality has been based, all too frequently, upon woman's disregard for the rights of her husband in her person.

For centuries the burden of sustaining a sexual moral standard has rested almost wholly upon the shoulders of the women; and it is therefore natural that the present-day defiant attitude of many women toward the traditional standard should be viewed with alarm; and there is more in this thought of alarm than the mere anxiety on the part of man to hold woman to her appointed task of guardian of marital morality.

Although men may wander from the home and fireside, it is a peculiar fact that they generally hold to a mental string by which they may find their way back again, very frequently the more contented to be there for their wanderings. But with a woman it is different. Once a woman has broken loose from the ties that have bound her to her inherited post of morality-preserver, she seldom goes back again, but keeps on her way until she finds that for which she seeks, or gives up the search of her own volition.

Is this, then, evidence that it is a woman's first duty to "stay put" when matrimonial exigencies have placed her in a specific "pocket" of the matrimonial billiard-table?

We believe not; and this belief is founded upon the fact that the female principle, which is, we admit, the centralizing, centripetal force in the cosmos, is not always manifested in the form of woman. The balanced individual is bi-sexual, even as the balanced "twain-one" is bi-sexual. If man was all male principle, and woman all female principle they would not be complementary, but antithetical. Each must be balanced within himself and herself before they can merge into each other.

Affinities are numerous, but mates are found but once; otherwise, the problems that are being discussed here would never have arisen.

If, then, as has been shown in the fact that only counterpartal unions are real, eternal and spiritually indissoluble, and that only true mates can thus unite, and when thus united have no desire to wander, what becomes of our ideas of sexual infidelity?

Since the very law of the Cosmos has seen to it that we cannot be untrue to the only one who seemingly has a right to our fidelity in the sex relation and since this union can become general only by freeing love from bondage, what becomes of the laboriously built up ethics of our social intercourse?

Are they to be abandoned as of no value?

We can almost hear the storm of protest which the righteous reader may feel in duty bound to let loose at such a suggestion, if for no other reason than that protest is the accepted way of proving one's own virtuous tendencies.

In the early seventies, a woman named Virginia Woodhull brought down upon her defenseless head the un-Christian-like abuse of the Christian public by announcing a doctrine which seems to have been nothing more dreadful than that of an equal standard of morality for men and women. The poor woman died broken-hearted, it is said; and yet nothing that we can unearth regarding her personal life and habits would seem to have warranted the cruel gibes that were hurled at her. The dear old lady lived a most continent, even ascetic life.

But the world has made rapid strides since that time, and we trust that the urgent need of something reasonable and feasible upon the sex question will inspire the reader to an unprejudiced review of this chapter. We would that it were possible to supply a modicum of understanding with each copy of this volume; but since it is not, we must take our chance with the average. Let us reason together:

Expediency is the mother of morality in social organizations, which have, of necessity, unstable, ever-changing standards. These standards represent, for some, ideals yet to be attained; while for others they become mere mileposts on the path of Evolution. The individual reaches, and then passes, an accepted ideal; gradually when a sufficient number, constituting a majority, have reached this ideal, it ceases to be a standard for the social organization, and another ideal is substituted.

The laws of the cave-man called for self-restraint exercised toward his own immediate clan, and this necessity for self-restraint was based upon nothing higher than the law of self-preservation; but gradually the sphere widened;

from clan to nation. So do our ethical and moral standards enlarge. Traditional concepts are not necessarily wrong, but they are almost sure to be <u>inadequate</u> to evolving Mankind.

Formerly, sexual morality consisted of the reservation of the person of a sister to the use of her brothers. Any infringement upon this moral code was punished by death to the woman and to her out-clannish lover.

And we have today an analogous example, although we are glad to say, it is not the highest standard; still, if one's husband or wife violates the marriage vows, it is more condonable, if the co-respondent be of the wealthy class; and in monarchies it is accounted an honor to have been selected as the king's favorite.

The institution of prostitution which exists everywhere today has its standards in the different countries; and the white races seem to think that their morality is superior to that of the Orientals because the social standing of prostitutes in the Orient is not irretrievably lost; they are permitted, in the event of marriage, to resume social equality with other women. Among white people, prostitutes have no other recourse than to sink lower and lower, until utter degradation is reached.

We believe that the Oriental view of the situation is a far higher standard of morality than is our Occidental attitude.

If there can lawfully be such an organization as is now being proposed as desirable in large cities, namely, a "morals police," it certainly should be instigated by a more sane purpose than that which is at the root of our present police guardianship.

Attempts at suppression of prostitution have hitherto been conducted on the principle that the women of that class are objectionable to the sight of our mothers and sisters and wives, and the sinfulness of the hopelessly "fallen" ones has been the theme of press and pulpit. And all the time the women of the half-world have resented this attitude as being unjust, and unfair, and hypocritical, and untenable. They have known that if the act of selling their bodies to men is a crime against the community, then more than half the feminine world is criminal. And they have contended that since the "respectable" women were neither contacted nor exploited by them, they cannot see wherein they offend society, provided the laws of sanitation and segregation are complied with.

In other words, they have said that it is none of Society's business whether they sell themselves to one man or to a number, since they must pay the penalty. And their attitude is relatively right. It is none of Society's business whether a woman is a prostitute or not, considered as an offense against

Society. That is the wrong attitude toward this condition of our social disorder.

No prostitute offends you or me. She, poor creature, offends herself, and we offend her and ourselves by permitting social conditions that make for such degradation. We are conniving with her to barter her birthright of freedom and real love for food and shelter, and taint and tinsel, whenever we encourage marriage on any other ground than that of true love, and when we regard virtue as a matter of physical contact.

If we judge from the many plays which we see on the boards; if we are influenced by the press and the pulpit; we must acknowledge that the general idea of sexual morality is an absurd one. The inference is that one special organ of a woman's physical body is the sole custodian of all virtue and all morality. The accepted idea seems to be that if a woman is married her body is then the property of her husband. Her emotions, her mind, her heart, her happiness, her preferences do not count for anything. The one act is made all-important. On the husband's side, if he provides for his wife and family, he is justified in exacting the sole right to the wife's body, and although his own heart and caresses may be given to another, he justifies himself, and the wife not infrequently feels satisfied, as long as he provides well for her. What is this but prostitution? The principle is the same as in the case of the recognized prostitute, although the conditions are easier for the woman, and less cheapening of her womanhood, but the difference is only in degree.

Now, a singular idea of fidelity, a direct antithesis to the one just mentioned, prevails among prostitutes, when married either by law or by selection.

They may surrender their physical body to another, for money, and according to their idea they may yet remain true to the husband or lover, because the matter is a business transaction. The other man has only what he has purchased, namely, the physical body. But should the woman permit another man to arouse in her a sexual response; should another invade her mind, absorb her thoughts, or engage her heart, the husband is outraged and the woman realizes her unfaithfulness.

All of which goes to show that up to the present time sexual morality has in itself no absolute uniform standard by which it can be measured and satisfactorily and convincingly presented to all persons, as have other phases of morality, such as honesty, justice, mercy, generosity, friendship, fidelity to country, and self-sacrifice to the good of humanity.

And although all these moral qualities have their bearing upon sexual morality, they do not establish a uniform ideal of sexual morality. Honesty is honesty whether in Paris, London, Calcutta, or Pekin, but as has been previously observed, sexual morality is determined by local conditions.

Can there, then, be established a universal standard of sexual morality? There can, but its universal acceptance is a remote probability, albeit it will arrive some day.

First of all, the sex relation must be absolutely free from sale; coercion; or barter; whether within the respectable "sale" of matrimony or of recognized prostitution. It must be free from any erroneous idea of marital duty; it must be exalted, reverenced, deified, in all its aspects, from the impregnation of a plant, to the sexual embrace of human lovers.

An Utopian dream it appears, if we note but one side of the picture. If we consider the lightness with which so many men look upon the physical form of women; and if we realize the attitude of so many women toward men, in their conflict with life, using the age-old dowry from mother Eve, of sex, as a weapon of defense and of offense; if we listen to the ribald songs that offend our ears and nauseate our souls, not only in music-halls and on the streets, but in supposedly cultured homes; and above all if we contemplate the uncleanness of mind displayed by those who are really in earnest in their endeavor to uplift the moral tone of the world.

These latter are, by far, the worst enemies to the Regeneration of Sex. A wise man once said, "Save me from my friends; I can protect myself against my enemies"—and so it is in this instance.

Most "Civic-Leaguers" and members of "Vice-Commissions" (why that name, anyway?) are infected with the bacteria of sex-degradation. They really require a lengthy process of mental disinfection, before attempting to handle so delicate a problem as this one of sexual uplift.

A woman member of a Young People's Civic League of the second largest city in the United States recently declared in public print, of the beautiful and chaste painting "September Morn," that it was "lewd, filthy, and suggestive of unclean things." This type of woman is intrusted with the task of teaching youthful minds; polluting them with the blasphemous affirmation that the Creation of the Father-Mother God of the universe is "lewd and filthy!"

Let us get this truth implanted in our mentality, as it is inrooted in our souls, namely:

Sex is always the purest, the holiest, and the most sacred thing in the universe —because God is Him-Her-Self, bi-sexual. The righteousness of it cannot be determined by so fickle a thing as man's customs; cannot be dependent upon mortal laws. This statement, indisputable as it is, will nevertheless start a chain of thought which may lead to confusion; and it is because of this tendency to confusion that the real issue is so frequently avoided. But let us see if we may not dispel the confusion by a system of logical deduction.

One thing is certain. The present condition of the Sex-problem is sadly chaotic. If we cannot hope to clarify it to the comprehension of the average, we may at least do so for some.

One of the first objections to the acceptance of the statement that the sex relation is, per se, always right, will be found in the conclusion to which the average mind immediately jumps: "Ah, then it is right for men and women who are depraved and licentious to live as they do; it is right for husbands and wives to deceive each other, and while pretending to be faithful to their marriage vows, to secretly carry on flirtations and intrigues with other men and other women!"

Ask one hundred men or one hundred women this question: "Is the sex-relation right or wrong?"

The men will declare that it is "right sometimes and wrong sometimes." The women, almost as a unit, will do the same. Occasionally a woman will be found sufficiently illumined to give a sane answer.

Following up the thoughtless answer with the request to illustrate, and the reply will be something like this: "Well, if people are married it is right, but if they are not married it is wrong;" and even as this silly answer is given, the person answering knows that it is puerile; but since the Public Mind prefers hypocrisy to Truth, few have the temerity, and fewer yet have the capability, to utter Truth.

It would be as sensible to say that it is right for the sun to shine sometimes and wrong for it to shine some other times. It is right for the sun to shine. This is all the answer that there is, and all that is needed.

Whether the sunshine bestows life and health, or decay and death, is entirely "up to us." The sun does its part. It is fulfilling the inexorable law of Nature, and is therefore right.

But of even greater importance in the universe is this law of sex. The law is forever and always right. Our concept of it may be right or it may be diseased. As a matter of fact it is, in all too many cases, diseased. If it were not, there would be no disease in the world.

How is it possible to have a perfect flower—a healthy, normal and wholesome sprout from a diseased root?

The root of all life is sex. We have thought disease into it, and the only remedy is to change our thought toward the function. This may be done by realizing that the sex-relation is always pure, holy, sacred—the bi-une God of the universe. This statement is quite different from saying that people are always right or sacred in their sex-relations.

To say that the sex-relation is always right under the institution of marriage and always wrong outside of it, is a lie. A lie cannot bring back health to either a person or a principle. Truth is the only thing that can make us whole —and the first office of Truth, as everyone knows, is to make us free. We cannot be whole until we are free, and the essential thought to be free from, is an attempt to keep alive the lie that the righteousness of Sex, per se, depends upon marriage.

Does the libertine believe in the sacredness of sex? Never. Does the prostitute claim for herself spotless purity? If she did, she would not sell herself for money.

Do men and women who are living in secret unfaithfulness hold exalted ideals of sex?

If they did, they would not maintain a life of deceit.

These people live as they do, because they have divorced sex from love. They agree absolutely with the blind "moralists" who regard Sex as a human playing—something which may be called bad one day and good the next, according to whether it is viewed from afar or near.

Does anyone imagine that when Society shall have established the "one standard of morality" replacing the double standard which now persecutes the woman only, for infringement upon Society's one demand, that of concealment, that the answer to sex-degradation will have been found?

A single standard is an improvement upon the old habit of stoning the woman only and letting the man go free. But why stone anybody?

History fails to record a single instance where Society has succeeded in improving either itself or its victims by the procedure. The best that can be said of the stoning habit is that it distracts attention from ourselves.

Persons who hold exalted ideas of the function of sex, realizing that a force so eternal and universal must be disassociated from man-made regulations, are not in danger.

Such as these will not foster deceit nor profligacy, any more than they will cringe and crawl under the lash of Society's disapproval, should they encounter it. They know that if they would find the highest good, they must serve Truth first of all, no matter how high the price of such devotion.

CHAPTER X

THE PATHWAY OF LOVE

Love is the Great Reality.

Everything else in this world of Experience is either tributary to love or it is an unsatisfying substitute for love; or a counterfeit of love. Love is the one cohesive, unifying, constructive force, and it is at the same time the only liberating force.

Hatred, as exemplified in warfare, may sometimes appear to free a people from the rule of a tyrant, but unless love be at the root of the "casus belli," other and more direful disasters will follow in the wake of seeming victory.

There is an erroneous idea, quite general among Christian people, that Death frees the spirit from the bonds that hold it to the mortal and the incomplete. Death only drops off the garment of the flesh; there are innumeral sheathings yet to be shed, before the soul grows the wings with which to soar to the celestial realms, where Love reigns supreme.

Love is the only power on earth or in the spheres, that can liberate us either from our own prejudices and hatreds and fears; or from the limitations and attractions of the animal-man.

Love is, indeed, the Alpha and Omega of Life. "There is no other God but Thee," has been the cry of every race on this globe, apostrophizing the unrecognized little baby-God, personified and presented to the race-mind as Horus; or as Krishna, or as Christ; but always it is Love, the Invisible, the Beautiful One, who is adored.

Ingersoll with his wonderful gift of word-painting, and inspired by that great love of humanity which characterized him, has said:

"Love is the only bow on life's dark cloud. It is the morning and evening star. It shines on the babe and sheds its radiance on the tomb. It is the mother of art; inspirer of poet, patriot and philosopher. It is the air and light of every heart; builder of every home; kindler of every fire on the hearth; it was the first dress of immortality. It fills the world with melody, for music is the voice of love. Love is the magician, the enchanter that changes worthless things to joy and makes right royal queens and kings of common clay. It is the perfume of that wonderful flower, the heart, and without that sacred passion that divine swoon, we are less than beasts, but with it—earth is Heaven and we are gods."

It would be superfluous to state here, that Love has ever been recognized as the supreme prize, lacking which all other gifts of life are worthless.

It is admitted that Love is almost the only thing in this age of commercial supremacy which can not be bought. Though it may be bartered for.

Although it be unreservedly admitted that Love is the all-powerful and magic solvent which transmutes all baser emotions into the higher, the general inference will be drawn that this type of love is not sexual. It will be termed parental; humanitarian, self-sacrificing, or altruistic love, and the point may be taken that if humanity had developed nothing higher than the love which is manifested in the sex instinct, the world would be a sorry one indeed, since sexual love, as we have witnessed its ascent from protoplasm to man, has been, in most instances, a blind urge toward personal gratification, not more lofty than the need of supplying the craving for food. This is quite true of animals, and of the lower types of animal-man; not necessarily the earliest types of men, but the lowest types, which we still have with us but happily in decreasing numbers.

But even among animals we find evidences of something vague, indefinite, but insistent which leads the animal to exhibit what we term a tendency toward *selection*; and in the animal also, through the exigencies of sexual love, we find parental love, and here again we note a peculiarity which ascends also into the family life of humans, namely, that in some instances what we have called the maternal love, the gentle, care-taking, guarding and protecting love, is demonstrated by the male. This is less common with the animals than with Man, but it is sometimes found and proves the existence of the evolutionary trend toward balance in the individual, as well as in the family.

If maternal love were confined strictly to the female parent, and the procreative instinct were the legitimate inheritance of the male only, we could never hope for a perfect sexual union, for the very cogent reason that the love of the male would never equal that of the female, since our capacity grows by becoming diffused.

As the world stands today, parental love takes a higher place in the life of the family, and of the nation and of the race (the family on a larger scale), than does love of husband or wife; and over and above even parental love we have been accustomed to place the love of God.

Now we know that there are many who claim that their love of this abstract God supercedes that of love for their family, but we may tacitly agree to take this statement as either an admission of fear of the Unknown or the realization that there are heights and depths of the love-principle which they have not yet penetrated, something to which the spirit soars. They intuitively recognize that there is some perfected state to which we aspire, else human love would never flower into its full possibilities.

And so when we declare that we love God above all other loves; more than wife or husband; children or parents; we are but admitting that we realize in our interior nature that we have not yet loved any *human being* with as great a love as we are capable of.

If any one holds the mistaken idea—and it is one that is very generally held—that the perfect sex union can be attained by no finer phase of emotion than that expressed in procreation; and that in order to develop the highest quality of sex-love, he must eschew all other phases of manifestation, and concentrate the forces of his being in the direction of sexual expression, he will meet with dire defeat. The laws of the cosmos cannot be broken. We are constantly confronted with the admonition, the child of Fear, to "be careful not to break the laws of God." We need not worry at all about the laws of God, whether we call these Cosmic Law, or Nature, or Divine Providence or something else. Our concern is with ourselves. Neither need we worry whether our neighbor obeys the moral code as we see it. So long as he does not refuse to us our right to follow our own ideals, we may permit him the same liberty.

God, as manifested in the cosmic law of transmutation, will take care of Him-Her-Self. Morality can not be extinguished. Love cannot be killed by men. We can only hurt ourselves in trying.

Love is neither fickle, capricious nor sly, notwithstanding tomes of seeming evidence to the contrary. Love is the most perfect mathematician in the universe. With whatsoever measure a man or a woman metes out love, with that same measure it is returned. Neither is Love blind. Love is depicted thus, because he is not concerned with appearances, but with realities. He is not gazing without, but within. He is doing his best, the poor little neglected Love-god, with the material at hand since he must fulfill the law of his being. He seeks to unite lovers in their interior nature, but as each of the would-be happy pair is bent on gazing without, instead of within, he is handicapped. And when unhappiness follows, they blame the blindness of Love, instead of realizing that He is depicted with a bandage over His eyes, to indicate that Love is an interior quality. So too, the Egyptian God Horus, the God of Love, was depicted with his finger on his lips, to typify the truth that true love is not noisy, blustering, jealous, burning, ranting, protesting. He is silent; soft; melting; blissful; magnetic; *uniting*.

Our noisy civilization, seeking happiness in Things, mistakes protestations and appearances for realities, and so modern marriages are consummated on this basis, and the caricaturists have depicted Cupid as having exchanged his love-darts for dollars, but this is a slander on the little god who wouldn't know a dollar if he could see one. "It is not true that one knows what one sees; one sees what one knows," declared a clever Frenchman, and as the average modern bride and bridegroom are forced, or think they are, by modern standards of living, to know dollars better than they know Love, their perverted vision sees Cupid's arrows tipped with the dollar mark. But even the dollar mark spells US, united, and if they are indeed truly united in love, wealth untold is theirs, and if they are not thus united then indeed are they poor in happiness, which is the only real poverty.

But even in the very failure to attain happiness in things, married couples have learned or they are learning, that there is an interior nature which must be considered if marital happiness is expected.

In all too many instances it may take many experiences and the road to the heights may for a time be lost but let us remember that "Love never faileth."

It has been said that "love makes gods of men," and we have taken this phrase as a charming bit of hyperbole, whereas it is a literal truth, because when two individual souls have rounded and balanced their natures by means of love, they come together in an eternal union, and are immortal; "in their flesh they have seen God," and the pilgrimage is ended.

There is a phrase current at the present day, belonging to slang, that universal language of the masses, "the Volapuk of the melting-pot." It comes to us simultaneously with the affinity-wave and the soul-mate quest; and it is both pertinent and timely, although by no means always wisely applied. It is the expression "I have found my seek-no-farther; he (or she) is the Real Thing."

Life is a succession of experiences in the quest of immortality. Immortality would be a curse instead of a blessing if attained alone.

Even the attainment of so unworthy an ambition as riches is a mockery if unshared by others. Fame is like a ruined and deserted castle to the one who has achieved it, unless there be the one other to share it. Even the philosopher, the philanthropist, the humanitarian, he whose love nature is supposed to find satisfaction in making others happy—can not realize the completeness and fullness of joy, unless there is the one mate with whom he may share his altruistic work; or lacking this, he looks to the Life Beyond for the completeness which he does not find here.

Renan says: "One reason why religion remains on such a material plane for many is because they have never known a great and vitalizing love; a love where intellect, spirit and sex finds its perfect mate."

Verily, love is the only vitalizing power in the universe; and when denied the interior union which should exist between a conjoining pair, Love does the best He can, and infuses into the relationship as much of the divine nectar as they will accept.

There is no impure love. I repeat: There is no impure love. The impurity is in the mortal mind of man, obstructing his vision until he fails to see the purity of that which fain would lift him from the Slough of Despond to the Heights of Bliss.

If love be always pure, if it be always the uplifting, unifying, constructive power of the universe, what becomes of the apparent fact that men have sinned for love of woman; that for love of man, women have lost their self-respect, their hope of Heaven; and have sunk to depths below that of the brute creation?

What becomes of the all too many instances where human nature appears to love vice; to be under the spell, as it were of a passionate love for all that is ignoble and defiling? How, then, can we say that love is always pure when it leads to such disaster?

Love never leads to disaster, though love may follow wheresoever the erring mind of man leads, and thus Love is all too frequently dragged from his true place of exaltation, and brought into the arena of human conflict. Love is no fighter; He never opposes; He only concurs; He unites if there is anything with which he can establish an affinity of union.

Egoism is the arch-enemy of love, selfishness is the manifestation of egoism. Selfishness seeks to possess; it is selfishness that causes a man to commit crime, in order that he may bedeck the woman he loves with jewels and fine raiment. He is buying her bodily presence with the baubles which he vainly believes will bind her to him; and he must be taught the lesson of the Yoga sutras "not this way; not this way;" and the more worthy he is of redemption, the more certainly will he be caught in the trap of his own making, lest he really perish; whereas by seeming defeat, outward defeat, he may learn the true path of inwardness. Certainly Love is the only guide to whom he may safely trust his redemption.

If a woman really sinks into the depths of degradation through what appears to be love, it is because selfishness and vanity have temporarily supplanted Love. But there is another side to the question. Society has very erroneous ideas of success and failure; and in looking at these opposite ends of the same pole, Society may be standing on it's head.

A story illustrative of this inverted view of success is worth repeating.

A young Englishman of aristocratic family, tired of the inanities of social life, and denied the privilege of entering the commercial world, emigrated to the South Seas. It was reported at home that he had married a native Samoan woman and was living the simple life of the Islanders. English society, when his name was mentioned at all, spoke of him with hushed voices and with a "what a pity y' know" manner as of one who had sunk below the depths of ordinary failure. Subsequently a friend visited Samoa and found the young man enjoying life and evidently supremely content. In the course of conversation the visitor chanced to speak of a mutual friend who had been rather wild in the days when they both knew him, and thinking to impart agreeable news to the exile, the visitor eagerly assured him that "Sir Arthur is respectably married and settled down now" whereupon the self-constituted exile commiseratingly responded with: "what a pity; and he was such a decent sort, too." So we may see that there is much in the point of view.

Happiness is the final test of success or failure; and we may trust this test, because no one can be happy in any other than the progressive, upward-trending life. Dissipation has never been a satisfactory substitute for happiness. Wealth is valueless to the possessor if it shuts out love; and if love be present, wealth holds but an inconsequential place.

However it be, the pathway of Love is long; and between the force of attraction which unites two atoms in chemical affinity, and the union of two perfected human beings, in whom Love and Wisdom are balanced, there are many degrees of the manifestation of Love, and the question inevitably arises "what shall we do with those marriages that are not yet perfect?"

If, as here premised, there is in the entire universe but one mate for each man and each woman; and if the union of perfect mates is the only truly spiritual union; if this union precludes the possibility of "temptation" in any other direction, what is to be done with all the marriages which we know to be imperfect; wherein it is evident that soul-union is not present? Are they immoral, and are they to be abandoned? And is marital infidelity in such instances immoral?

It is. Infidelity is always immoral, because all deceit and deception and dishonesty are immoral.

Let us see what constitutes infidelity, irrespective of marriage. Infidelity is to be unfaithful to a trust imposed; to betray a confidence; to break a promise. This is the abstract definition and it is the only definition that will withstand analysis, whether applied to the marriage vows or to other promises and pledges.

Obviously the answer to this question, then, is to either not impose upon oneself or upon another "vows"; or, if we do so impose, not to break them; but if vows are not to be broken, they may, thank Heaven, be dissolved.

And surely the marriage ceremony of the future will not impose vows or promises, because intelligent men and women must rise superior to the necessity for bonds and promises. A marriage ceremony is, even at its very highest, when the contracting persons are spiritually mated, nothing more than announcement to the society of which they are members, of the fact of their mutual agreement to live outwardly, as well as inwardly, in sexual union.

We make too much of the marriage ceremony and too little of the fitness for marriage. The business of the clergyman is altogether too much confined to seeing whether a couple is "respectably" bonded, and altogether too little as to whether they are spiritually united.

Possession! that is the word that spells unhappiness, in married life; each wants to possess the other; neither one tries for the spirit of union. Possession cannot be divorced from deceit.

Vows and promises challenge us to keep them, and because our pathway leads upward to freedom, we constantly find these vows and promises staring us in the face and daring us to advance. We must substitute mutual confidence for vows. Vows are childish and puerile. If we cannot keep faith without vows then are we sadly lacking in faith and should cultivate it by offering to others the freedom of action we would have ourselves. When the time comes, as it will, that a husband and wife can "talk it over" in a friendly, mutually helpful frame of mind, when either one is attracted by another, there will be no further opportunity for infidelity; and the sooner we rid the world of a belief in sin and immorality, the sooner will Love reign.

It is said of the sages of India that they can live in the jungles and the ferocious tigers will not harm them; how do they accomplish this?

They have disassociated themselves from ferocity. They do not desire to crush or kill the tiger. Their minds are so filled with love and compassion that there is no point of connection between them and the destructive instinct in the beast.

When we get away from the fear of "impure" love; when we get away from the tremendous load of belief in evil which keeps the back bent and the eyes lowered to the dust, we will be ready to meet the pure and perfect love when it comes; and when we are fit for it we will meet it and when we have found this pearl of great price, all doubt and fear, all jealousy; all dissatisfaction will vanish. There will be no fear of "losing" each other. The union is an interior one, and even though "seas divide and mountains vast, rear their proud crests 'tween thee and me," the call of soul to soul will be felt and answered. Byron says:

> "There are two souls of equal flow,
>
> Whose gentle streams so calmly run,
>
> That when they part—they part? Oh no,

They cannot part, those souls are one."

With a sentiment such as this between two beings, what need for vows and promises, and bonds?

It is customary for writers on the sex question to emphatically, even feverishly, emphasize the fact that they have no intention of implying that they would do away with the bonds of matrimony; and although this conclusion is inevitable where one's intellect is active and the faculty of deduction brought into play, yet the false modesty that prevails and the prejudices that blind the eyes of the multitude, and above all, the tendency of the undeveloped race-mind to impute personal motives to such as would, if permitted, lead them to a freer, and consequently a purer life, impel the writer to deny that which is, finally, the very point at issue.

In the interest of Truth, we are compelled to state that we would do away with "bonds." We would substitute therefor mutual agreements, subject to renewal or repudiation within certain defined and mutually helpful conditions. Vows and bonds and oaths are the crutches of the crippled human race. We need not always walk lame.

It may be argued that man is still largely animal; yes, but the surest way to keep him so is to treat him like an animal. If we remind him that he is also a man and that he may be a god; and if we point out to him the way in which he may accomplish this transmutation, no man has so little intelligence that he will not attempt to follow, when assured that God-hood means a bliss so great that he can hardly imagine it; that it means cessation of the "endless round of births and deaths" from which Gautama, the Buddha, sought to free himself. Mankind has always been promised immortality through spiritual union— with what? An abstract principle called God, or Aum or any other impersonal formless all-inclusive Being?

No, but with his mate.

On this point we trust that there will not remain any obscurity. There is no higher God than Love. There is no higher love than sexual-love in its highest manifestation. The more we truly love, the more love flows into and through our consciousness, until from a tiny little pearly drop of the "wine of life" we ascend to the Olympian Heights and imbibe floods of the "nectar of the Gods."

Even the libertine, that pauper in the realm of Love, wants the perfect life. His soul is forever hungry for that which he gropingly tries to catch and chain and possess; and which by virtue of these same desires will evade him until he ceases thus to seek, and instead of demanding possession of the object of his desires, he asks for union. Union is interior; possession is always and ever limited to exterior contact. They who would enter the sanctuary and defile the "Holy of Holies" are saved from such a load of self-inflicted sin; they cannot if they would. There is but one key which will open the golden gate to heaven. The way chosen by the libertine is in exactly the opposite direction.

Are all marriages that are not soul-mate unions immoral? Most certainly not. Are all unions that are not married immoral. Most certainly not.

We have made an attempt to define sexual immorality and we have concluded that as yet there is no absolute standard in civilized or uncivilized ethics, since, as Letourneau points out, what is immoral in Pekin or Calcutta may be moral in Paris or London. Truth is adherence to facts in whatever section of the world. Tolerance; sympathy; charity; may be clearly defined wherever we roam. Sexual immorality has no stable standards. We here suggest one and submit that it is the only one possible of universal concurrence. It is based upon personal freedom. Wherever the sexual relation is made a convenience; or where either one marries in the face of his or her own realization that there is no love bestowed, that relationship is immoral. Thus, it will be seen that sexual immorality is independent of marriage, and cannot be estimated by law. Marriage for money; for position; for convenience; for anything other than a desire for mutual helpfulness, is immoral. Indulgence in the sexual act for selfish gratification without regard to the welfare of each other; for money; or pastime; or for any motive other than a reverential expression of an unselfish love, is immoral and is a prostitution of the divine office of sex.

But, though not all sex relationships can be perfect and eternal, yet all may, if we desire, be moral. And all moral and sexual relationships must, and will, lead to perfect sex-union, whenever the time comes that either one is ready for the completement. This truth need not, and will not, disrupt any happy marriages.

If the Church had not made the mistake of teaching the fallacy that sex-love is a strictly earthly or mortal function, divorcing Sex from pure love; and if the Theology had not tried to substitute the love of, and union with, an abstract Creator for love of mates in soul-union, perhaps there would be exhibited less impatience of the restraints of marriage.

But with a cat-and-dog married life on the one hand and the prospect of an inane, blank, and sexless union with an abstract God-idea on the other, it is small wonder that mortal consciousness has rebelled, and has decided to take its chances with Hell, rather than to forego the happiness which is intuitively sensed as being the direct prerogative of perfect mating.

If this God-idea had not been presented as an eternal, unescapable finality, there might have been hope; but to fly about a throne endlessly, night and day, singing, "I want to be nothing; nothing; only to lie at His feet"—the prospect appalls!

Small wonder that the conclusion has been deduced that "life is too short" for anything like domestic misery, when domestic happiness is the only happiness we know, and that is to cease at death!

But, if we take the truthful view of marriage and of heaven; if we realize that mortal life is Experience; that as we learn by experience, we acquire knowledge; as we accumulate knowledge, we begin to glimpse wisdom; and that when we have sufficient Wisdom and sufficient Love, we graduate into the classification of God-hood, immortality; and that immortality means union with our mate; sex-union, in all that constitutes its highest and most satisfying aspect as we know it, with infinitely more of beauty and love and bliss, there is an incentive to aspire.

Love is the only way that immortality can be attained. It cannot be "taken," like degrees of secret societies. It cannot be purloined, or feigned. Fear has never made people good. The doctrine of punishment has never deterred the sinner. Even in his apparent acceptance of the doctrine of sin and of consequent punishment, the poor sinner has known better. Humanity has progressed in spite of the fear that has dwarfed our stature.

In the new day, with hope ahead and fear transmuted into a wise patience, this earth may yet be a "fit dwelling-place for the gods."

Leigh Hunt says: "Love is a personal proof that something good and earnest and eternal is meant us; such a bribe and foretaste of bliss being given us to keep us in the lists of time and progression; and when the world has realized what love urges it to obtain, perhaps death will cease and all the souls which love has created crowd back at its summons to inhabit their perfected world."

We are prone to consider such statements as only so many beautiful words— elusive, ethereal, and descriptive of something that is always in the future; but if it be always in the future it will never be ours; we cannot catch up with it; and thus it becomes a mockery. These prophetic utterances are literal truths.

Let us confide to you a little secret: We are as much spirit now as we will be when death has unloosed the bindings of our disguise—the body. The real of each of us is what we are now, in our interior nature.

While we are building the business which sustains our physical body; while we are studying law or medicine or philosophy or religion or whatsoever, we are at the same time developing the interior nature which we are now, and which we will be when the life of the body ceases. Not all business men are alike, and yet, if business were their only reality, they must needs be all the same for employing the same methods. Not all doctors are alike although they graduate from the same school of medicine. The inner entity that we are, stands or falls in the final test, by the motives; the desires; the sentiments; the sympathies; the generosities; the forgiveness; the kind impulses; the pities; the charities; the tolerances; we feel while we are apparently engrossed in the outer life. Together, these little impulses, perhaps forgotten in the rush of the day's seemingly important business affairs, come finally to be the ladder by which we climb to the spiritual heights where the bliss of true and perfect, melting, merging, liquid-love, of the one and only mate awaits us.

One thing more. This also is a secret. Perhaps you will not even believe it, but it is true: Poets are the practical members of our crazy civilization. Business men are practical only when they are also, and above all, idealists.

CHAPTER XI

THE LAW OF TRANSMUTATION

External life is a succession of picture blocks with which we have builded our thoughts into shapes and forms manifest to the mortal senses. But back of every act there is the invisible ideal which prompted it, so that to the one who has the interior vision; one who looks at life from the citadel of his own interior nature instead of merely sensing it by external contact, every material thing tells its interior story; everything has an esoteric or occult meaning. It is said that mystic truths have been veiled in symbolical language; but to those who know the language of symbolism, there is no veil; what seems so is due to the refractory character of the mind which is limited to sense consciousness.

There are two words much used in this day of the Dawn which give the key to the trend of the cosmic cycle upon which the earth has entered. The word "union," or its equivalent, enters into almost every phase of our busy life as well as into ethical and philosophical thought. This word, with much that it stands for, has superseded the word "agreement," or "combination" or "partnership," formerly used. Union means something more interior, than do these other words, even when applied to commercial issues.

The business man says to his partners "let us unite on this question." They are already partners, but unless there is a unity of thought and ideals, their partnership is an unsatisfactory and unfruitful one. We have labor unions which are intended to suggest a solidarity of effort; a merging of interests; a welding together into one thought-force, of those who enter the organization. The fullness of meaning of this word "union" is not adequately expressed in the words lodge, or club, or any of the terms used to designate an organization of men in social or commercial combination.

In union there is strength; but in partnership, or in clubs, there may be no quality of union, although there is the outward bond of fellowship. "I shall look into this" we say when we want to know more of a subject than appears on the surface. We want to know the within. We want to fathom the interior meaning; to get below the surface, or the appearance of it. This is the other word of vital import—the word *within*. We see it everywhere like a signpost directing our footsteps toward home.

The Master Jesus said that the immortal kingdom was within, but the Christian world evidently has not believed Him. He also told those who would listen to Him, that there was but one commandment that was truly spiritual, but as he did not come to destroy anything that existed, but only to transmute it, He paid no attention to the commandments already in vogue, but contented Himself with a repetition of the one and only commandment of the Father-Mother God Principle which begat him: "That ye love one another."

Now we are being told from the housetops and from the streets and through all the channels of the physical senses to look within. That which you are— not what you appear to be to the eyes of the sense-conscious—but that which you are in your interior nature, is what counts to you. The writer who writes because he is paid to write salable stuff, harps upon the necessity for "efficiency" in the commercial game; but when the word is impartially considered efficiency consists in the long run in reliability, and reliability is measured by one's honesty; integrity; square-dealing; wise judgment— interior qualities all. It matters not whether the skin be white or black or brown or yellow or green; whether you are of imposing stature or but four feet tall; it is what you are within that constitutes true efficiency.

So the kingdom whatever it may be whether of heaven or hell; of love; or of power; or of ambition; the kingdom is within. The source of your power is in the interior of your nature.

If we go to slang, which offers the line of least resistance to the Cosmic Law, we find that the cue has been given over and over again to those who are interiorly awake to receive it. "You are not in on this," has been said to one who was left out of some supposedly desirable thing; or "you are not *in* it," meaning that you are not up to the required standard. Even as the walls of a building only imperfectly indicate the nature of that which is within, that which the building stands for; that which it symbolizes, so physical appearances are symbolical hieroglyphs of the inner nature.

"Learn to look into the hearts of men" admonishes the spiritual teacher. "As a man thinketh in his heart so is he." The character of the heart is the test, and though a man's lips utter words that are at variance with his inner nature, yet if we have learned to look within, we are not deceived. This then is the key to the kingdom—interior vision.

Words are like buildings; like personalities; they have their exterior and their interior message. Knowledge may be accumulated; piled up like a mountain of possessions. But knowledge may not bestow one grain of true wisdom. It is only as we extract the interior message from knowledge that we attain wisdom. We possess knowledge and we *find* wisdom, when we have transmuted that knowledge into its interior meaning.

The fundamental difference between mysticism and theology is a difference founded upon this axiom. The true mystic penetrates to the interior nature of manifestation and gets the message of Experience. Mysticism excludes nothing. It includes the manifest with the interior; it penetrates the outer and seeks the interior; but never does the true mystic confound the spirit with the letter; never does he mistake the external for the Reality; the symbol for the message.

Suppose that what is generally called the practical side of life were the only reality. What would be the inevitable conclusion of the thinker if he were to consider only the outer, the manifest, the visible results of a given achievement? He would conclude that civilization is insane.

If we did not know with an intuitional grasp of truth that all this which we call "marvels of achievement" is symbolical of what Man is in his interior nature, it would be the veriest folly. What, for example, is there in a modern sky-scraper indicative of man's advanced civilization?

With millions of acres of unused land, it would be inconceivable folly to project into the inoffensive atmosphere twenty-eight stories of wood and iron merely to buy and sell the products of man's brain and hands. But while our Twentieth Century feverish activities are ostensibly engaged in the external world, they are symbolizing, embodying, teaching if we will but learn, the fact of the evolution of man's interior nature. Sky-scrapers are indicative of the heights to which we are aspiring; to which we are climbing; air-ships only tell us that man in his interior nature—in his reality—is not a creeping, crawling Thing, chained to the earth. He may, if he will, soar into ethereal realms. He has wings, and if he so desires, he may use them.

Wireless telegraphy would be a much less consequential discovery, did it not foreshadow the coming time when mind will speak to mind regardless of desert wastes and imponderable mountains that seemingly intervene. Wireless messages are the result of vibrations set in motion by means of a dynamo and received by an instrument attuned to a corresponding rate of motion. But no dynamo ever invented has the power that is centered in the dynamic will of a human being. Brute strength is paralyzed into inactivity by the comparatively puny strength of a man. The fierceness of the lion, the tremendous force of the elephant, give way before the potent power of Man's desire—an interior quality.

Do skyscrapers, or air ships, or wireless telegraph systems make us happier? If they do, is it not because of their ethical rather than their so-called practical value? Is it not because they prove to man his power to use the plastic material of the planet and control it to do his bidding? Rapid transit adds to convenience; but above and beyond all the so-called practical valuation which can be put upon modern inventions and accomplishment is the message which these mechanical marvels present to the mind. The message that man is not a machine; that he is not a creature but a creator; that he is not a miserable worm of the dust, but a winged god.

Greater than all the other benefits bestowed by modern mechanical marvels is the knowledge of each other which has resulted from intercommunication between nation and nation. The great breeder of discord and the waste of hatred is the idea of segregation. The man of the cave and the club feared his next door neighbor, because he did not know him, and the animal-man fears that which he does not know; his imagination pictures the unknown one as something monstrous and dangerous. Intimacy will teach us that people of a distant country are like ourselves, even though they may dress differently; even though they may wear their hair an inch longer or shorter; may eat a diet of nuts instead of meat; may pray standing up rather than kneeling down. Upon such trifling and absurd differences as these are based our ideas of "alien" races and "foreign" nations.

Annihilation of space and time accomplished by modern mechanical inventions has made us familiar with the interior life of other human beings and has compelled us to the knowledge that they have feelings, emotions, desires, hopes, aspirations, and faults, exactly like our own, and thus will be established a bond of unity, which will reach the heart of our neighbor. If this bond of unity has not as yet been established, it is because the majority of Mankind are still only sense-conscious. They have not yet assimilated the knowledge which the past few years has precipitated in such an avalanche that the slow-moving mind cannot keep pace with it. But out of all this knowledge must come in due time the quality of wisdom. Wisdom seeks love as the only eternal reality. Not because God has commanded that we shall do so; not because of a sentimental ideal, but because any other course is futile, foolish, silly and does not "get us anywhere" as the slangologists rightly express it.

Thus everything in the busy commercial world, seemingly bent upon perpetuating external forms and systems, is in reality a symbolic language of which "unity" and "within" are the pivotal centers. These two words are really complementary, because it is only with the interior nature that unity can be established.

We may conjoin; combine; contact; cohere. We may form partnerships, corporations, combinations from the outside. These are external expressions of the interior desire for unity, but union is of the interior nature only.

With the more intimate knowledge of each other which intercommunication between nations makes general, each little segregated mass of human beings must sooner or later arrive at the conclusion that we are very much alike and that to "get together" on any proposition involving the welfare of all humanity is a much less costly and a far more satisfactory way of settling matters than by going to war over it. Not that this idea is yet fixed in the brains of the majority, but there is creeping into man's cranium a faint thought that perhaps the survival of the fittest will be best maintained by peaceful methods; an idea that honor can neither be maintained nor appeased by shedding blood. This knowledge will bring us to the wise observation that fundamentally, cosmically there is no place for enmity between nations and races and classes and the sexes; that the whole conglomerated mass of hatreds and inherited enmities and segregated interests; the absurd idea that one part of the world can permanently prosper by the enslavement of any part; the undeveloped and savage ideas that underlie our civilization; all these thought-concepts have no more reality in the cosmic scheme of things, than have the picture-blocks of the child in the adult life.

The world has been living through a nightmare. The warfare which belongs to the animal plane of Man's evolving consciousness has been carried into the mental world as well. Not only do men fight like tigers in the jungles, but they fight with tongue and pen as well, using food products, textile fabrics, inventions, mechanical devices and the creations of brains of men, for their weapons. But this type of warfare will not much longer survive. Mankind must choose between transmutation or annihilation. Hatred is self-destructive. Blind indeed must be those who can expect to escape this law. "They who use the sword shall perish by the sword." How else can it be? There is but one force. If we use it to construct, we are constructed. If we use it to destroy we are destroyed, since it is by the very nature of law that we become involved in that which we employ. It is a simple sum in arithmetic. We may either add or subtract. If we add, there is no limit. If we subtract we ultimately wipe off the slate.

The fact is dawning upon an increasing number of thinkers, that even as brain is superseding brawn in the marts of the world, so there is still a finer and higher and better force, so potential in its power that nothing can withstand its melting, merging, unifying motive. That power is love, without which though we have all else we are but as "sounding brass and a tinkling cymbal."

Even as the ferocious man-eating animals have disappeared from the earth; even as the giant gladiators, the mailed knights, the erotic pomp and regalia of Imperialism, with their captives chained to their chariot-wheels; the cruel despots, the tyrannical masters and scourged slaves; the bloody sacrifices, the horrible games of the amphitheatres, even as these one-time evidences of alleged "civilization" have passed away, so too will time see the dissolution of our own "false gods." Transmuted into pure and perfect love and peace and equality, the power now misapplied in the work of hate and destruction, will increase a thousand fold and be directed toward the maintenance of a balanced world—a world in which Love and Wisdom are united.

We are always fearful of changes. The bat-like eyes of the multitude are blinded by the light of the sun. Why cannot we trust the Cosmic Law which has always given us a better ideal in the place of the decadent one? If we prefer to use the word God, then let us say why cannot we trust God?

In the external world, then, the idea that a part of this sphere is inherently antagonistic to another; that men are born enemies; that the female and the male must forever struggle for supremacy—all these ideas are disappearing. "Unity" is the password to the coming civilization. If then we will accept this conclusion and apply it to our individual selves, we will conclude that no function of the human organism should merit disapproval; or be regarded as an enemy. Before we can arrive at a balanced and sane world without, we must come to a balanced and sane state within our own organism.

We must know that the sex function, the most vital of all the various expressions of life in the individual body as well as in the social body and the racial body, is not an enemy with whom we must maintain unceasing warfare, but a wise and trustworthy friend with whom we may safely co-operate, neither repressing this vital force until we have conquered it and dragged it like a bleeding captive behind our chariot-wheels, nor should we like the drug-slave become lost in the clutches of an abnormal appetite.

Indeed, as the forces of life become transmuted from the physical appetites to the finer, and interior desires of the soul, abnormalities and perversions of sex-force will be impossible.

Sex-force is, at the Center of Being, unpolluted. It is pure, perfect and harmonious. It is divine. Why? Because it is bi-une; it is balanced.

In our present-day lopsided civilization, we find that nearly every one is lop-sided, and unbalanced. Alienists declare that almost every man and woman has some hobby or mania. Doubtless this is true. An age of specialization would incline the race toward "lopsidedness." But the source of Life is balanced; if we come to the place where we consciously unite with that interior source we will no longer be unbalanced, because the central source of life is Sex, and Sex is, at the center of the radius, bi-une, which is to say balanced. There is no chance for sex supremacy, for domination, or dispute, or jealousy. There is equilibrium.

It is probable that to those who cannot compass the consciousness that equality does not mean identicalness this sort of balanced life will appear tame and tasteless. Few women perhaps and certainly fewer men can imagine a sex-union in which love is so great, so over-powering and at the same time so perfect, that there is no room for jealousy. The average person believes that jealousy is inseparable from sex-love. But even as our antediluvian ancestors could not imagine the mechanical miracles of the telephone and the telegraph, so we fail to comprehend the infinite depth and intensity of our interior being until we come to the place where we awake from the sleep of the mortal and glimpse the heights of the immortal life.

No one can give to another this interior wisdom—this philosopher's stone, by means of which all baser instincts are transmuted into the pure golden-tinted light of illumination. He can but point the way and promise that the results are mathematically proportionate to effort, and effort will be backed by individual desire.

We do not hold, as do many writers dealing with the physiological side of the subject of Sex, that the sex function is primarily designed for purposes of procreation and that any other expression of sex is contrary to nature. The essential function of sex is to vitalize. Procreation is one of the uses of sex-love, but it is not its primary function.

Until men and women have absolute control over their sex impulses they are still on the plane of sense-consciousness; and as long as they remain only sense-conscious they miss the very thing that they seek. All that is pleasureable in sex-contact that reaches any man or woman who is only sense-conscious is no more than a faint echo of the ecstacy of divine and perfect love which is known to the spiritual alchemist, who has discovered the art of transmutation and thus found the key to the gate of eternal life.

As long as we remain limited to the plane of sense-consciousness, old age is a blessing. It compels transmutation of the love-nature into interior channels. By the failure of the physical organism to express the sex-desires, this force is given an opportunity to become transmuted into higher, finer and more intense and beautiful thoughts. It takes on whatever quality of soul we have acquired and it fosters that quality—be it much or little—so that we may not go into the interior realms a spiritual pauper.

Even as our physical childhood is a prelude to mental adultship, so old age, our "second childhood," is a prelude to our soul adultship, and the character of our old age period is prophetic of our state in the soul life.

There are some extremely aged persons whom we cannot, if we have any degree of interior vision, classify as old; the youth and beauty and love-radiance of their interior nature is so potent that it shines through the worn and wrinkled garment that covers it; and we know that when that garment shall have been removed by the hands of Death, that the soul will be clothed in radiant youth and beauty, and light.

This is indeed the esoteric cause of the widespread repudiation of a mental recognition of age.

"I am seventy years young" says the man who hopes for eternal youth and life; and if he says it from the standpoint of wisdom—the wisdom that knows himself an immortal soul fired by pure and holy spiritual love, then indeed his words are truly symbolical.

But if he utters them merely in desperate defiance of organic decay, they are empty and he will enter the after-life, even as he leaves this one, without having attained that which he craves.

This truth is an integral part of the cosmos, from which there is no appeal; no reprieve; no immunity, no "respecter of persons." The law is absolute and it is also just. Pure and perfect love is the price of immortal life. There is no other "coin of the realm."

"But," questions the initiate, "why cannot those who know, if there be such in the world today, give us this mystical formula? Why do they not tell us how we may reach this desirable state of spiritual sex-love, which affords such divine happiness to those who find it?" The query is pertinent and the desire is natural; the doubt of its reality is consistent, yet we are constrained to say that in the very nature of such inquiry the disciple of the Hidden Wisdom voices his unreadiness for *Illumination*. The desire for self-gratification, though right and natural to the sense-conscious plane, is yet inimical to attainment of spiritual consciousness.

There is a spiritual message in the persistently inculcated doctrine of sacrifice. It is not that a Supreme Being desires sacrifice, or gifts, or adulation, or homage, or worship, or that any power glories in our unhappiness. It is not that we may purchase any spiritual thing by giving up something which we prize, but it is because our spirit becomes attuned to the central source of Life by means of our willingness to perform what to the sense-conscious plane of existence seems a sacrifice.

"He sought for others the good he desired for himself; let him pass on" is the Egyptian phrasing of the Golden Rule, and this states it as clearly as it can be stated.

Yet should any one take this truism as an unfailing formula and expect to enter the golden gate of eternal life because of obedience to the letter of the pass-word, he would fail. Altruism *is*; it is not mere recognition of a word.

We may presuppose another natural and instinctive query: "If then only by union with one's true mate one can enter the bliss of eternal life and love, should not we drop every other responsibility, sever all ties of relationship, give up wife or husband or family or work, and search for the one perfect complementary, finding which, is found the answer to all life's problems?"

Again we can only say that the seeker would be disappointed. We should remember the story of Sir Launfall. Returning from the unfruitful quest of long years for the Holy Grail (the golden chalice), he learned the lesson of Truth from the beggar at his own door to whom he gave the cup of cold water *without any consciousness of doing a good deed*; without hope of thereby finding the grail.

He who seeks with the selfish thought of securing for self any good will not find it though he should give away every farthing to the poor; though he should never permit one unkind word to pass his lips; though he should fast and scourge and deny the flesh; kneel all day and all night in prayer. As long as he holds to the thought of self and of *obtaining* something so long will he miss the *attainment*.

Spiritual insight establishes two facts beyond cavil or dispute or reversion. One is that God's laws cannot be broken. We are not trying to say that they should not be broken; or that they cannot be broken with impunity; or that if broken we shall be punished. They simply cannot be broken—they are unbreakable.

We cannot buy or sell or beg or steal or borrow or take as a gift, or in any wise acquire immortal godhood, except by attaining it any more than we can come to physical manhood or womanhood except by growing to it; and by the same law no one can keep it from us; neither priest nor scribe; neither prophet nor inventor. We are a law unto ourselves. No one can break the law of your being any more than you can break that of another. No power on earth or in the celestial spheres or in the intervening spaces can keep that which is our own from us. Wherefore then, should we tear ourselves and each other with strife and jealousy and wounded honor and outraged marriage vows, when either partner to a marriage contract sees fit to sever that relationship?

If you lose out in what you believed to be love, be sure that the object of your desires was not yours to lose; in all the spheres there is only one who is yours by divine right and no one can by any possibility usurp your place in the final issue; and that place once found no one can oust you from it. But remember what we have said in previous chapters of the word "found;" it is from within.

How vain and how foolish it is to think that a power so stupendous, so magnificent and so beneficent as to project this immense panorama of life; to establish such marvelous diversity within such simple unity; to bestow the bliss of love, could make a mistake. How puerile has been the teaching that we can sin against the Eternal God. We need not worry about the Supreme and Eternal Power. "The dice of God are loaded." Our concern is with ourselves, lest we imagine that we may cheat in the game of life.

We are self-centered, free-willed; immune from any possibility of offending the universe. The whole problem of life and death, in so far as it relates to our individual selves, is "up to us." We can delay arrival at the goal of our desires; we can dally by the wayside if we will. Only our own loss, our own suffering, our own unsatisfied longing shall punish us. But who is so stupid that he would remain wandering in the bleak and barren desert, when he might by a turn of his hand enter fields Elysian and merge his soul into the boundless areas of infinite bliss and wisdom?

We should not imagine that death will do this for us. Death is nothing more phenomenal than withdrawing from one room to another. The soul may strive on for ages through many incarnations. Only one thing can free it; and that is love; love for others than the personal self. The broader and deeper the love nature, the wider it reaches out to enfold in its tender protection all living things, the more nearly divine we become, and the sooner will we touch the area of the spiritual and attract our own.

It is evident that self-seeking even for so worthy a possession as one's own counterpart defeats the very effort. We are not to seek; we are only to prepare ourselves to be ready and worthy; when we shall have done this, nothing can withhold our own from us; not though the two halves of the One Being are separated by all the barriers which the sense-conscious race of men have erected between themselves and the bliss of Heaven. Says Emerson: "What is thine, will gravitate to thee." We need not therefore go about apprehensively fearful lest we lose that which belongs to us; in so doing we are apt to keep our eyes glued to the earth, thus forgetting that it is from the higher realms of vibration "whence cometh our light."

Says Emerson: "O, believe as thou livest, that every sound that is spoken over the round world which thou oughtest to hear will vibrate on thine ear. Every proverb, every book, every by-word that belongs to thee for aid or comfort, shall surely come home through open or winding passages. Every friend whom not thy fantastic will, but the great and tender heart in thee craveth, shall lock thee in his embrace. And this because the great and tender heart in thee is the heart of all; not a valve, not a wall, not an intersection is there anywhere in nature, but one blood rolls uninterruptedly, an endless circulation through all men as the water of the globe is all one sea, and truly seen its tide is one."

Here then are specific and trustworthy statements for the further enlightenment of the student of the problems of Sex. Like algebraical propositions they prove themselves when correctly solved. Immortal godhood is attained by counterpartal union, because the Central Source of Life is bi-

120

une. Immortality is our spiritual birthright, but we must claim it if we would consciously realize this truth.

God is the bi-une creative principle, and we are literally and in truth the "image and likeness" of this bi-une Being. Not one hermaphroditic personality but a pair. A pair is one whole, even though each of the pair is distinct in form and diverse in temperament and qualities. We are especially emphatic upon this point because there has been so much vague and speculative theorizing upon this definition of a bi-une Being. Your perfect mate is distinctively masculine or distinctively feminine in sex as the case may be; and he or she is your mate because of this perfection of distinctiveness.

Our former ideas of femininity and of masculinity were faulty. Woman is not less but much more womanly, if she has exchanged fear for courage; deceit for truthfulness; ill-health for vitality; helplessness for helpfulness. Even as a man is more manly when he spares the nesting birds where formerly he ruthlessly destroyed; when he unites protection with bravery; when he knows sympathy from weakness; when he combines sentiment with principle; and gentleness with vigor.

No mortal can by any possibility break the laws of God. Therefore you are not to try to enforce your ideas of morality upon others. Who has constituted you book-keeper for the universe? You are to concern yourself with establishing happiness upon this earth.

You are to see to it that your love is big and broad enough; all-inclusive enough to wish to see every one happy from your immediate family to your far-off neighbor in Central Africa. You need not worry about whether they break the moral code as you see it. You are to render love and service to this world with all your heart and all your power; if you do this, you will reach the goal of your desires.

No mortal can by any other method than love and the service that is rendered through love seek and find the "Holy Grail," which is to say the bliss of spiritual union with his Beloved. Therefore to fly from the responsibilities and the environment in which you are, without regard to the welfare of others, is to defeat your own quest; neither do we claim that you should under all circumstances remain chained to a post like an unwilling captive, poisoning your mind with resentment and hatred.

There is no one formula which fits all cases—other than that given in love and service. The Golden Rule which tells us to do unto others as we would have them do unto us, has another side to its shield, and it may read "Do not permit others to do unto you what you would not do to them." If you seek freedom from a specific environment from no other motive than personal selfishness, you may be doing yourself an injury; but if you are also doing an injury to others by remaining, then you are doubly mistaken in your course.

The way of attainment is not easy, although the formula is simple; it may be briefly but concisely summed up in the vital and important word "unselfishness." "Not mine but thine also," is the watchword of the wise in love. Not possession of the Beloved One, but union with him or her. There is just one big world of difference between these two points of view. More than that, there is the difference of Heaven and Hell.

CHAPTER XII

"SELLING THE THRONES OF ANGELS"

Great as may seem to the sense-conscious person the pleasure and satisfaction of owning some one, or some thing; of possessing and feeling a proprietorship in the one desired; greater by a million-fold is the pleasure of union which is possible only to those who are themselves free, and who in consequence desire freedom for all others. This is a truth which the unwise cannot comprehend or concur in, and which they will not believe or trust.

Emerson says: "Every personal consideration that we allow costs us heavenly state. We sell the thrones of angels for a short and turbulent pleasure."

And finally, as regards the sex-function, we would like to impress upon every one, though only those who are fit for the kingdom will understand the truth, namely that the highest manifestation of sex-love is not localized in the organs of procreation. The love that is of the soul fills the breast first of all, and is only felt in the region popularly, but erroneously, supposed to circumscribe the sex-function, as a secondary and by no means compulsory consideration.

When the sex force has become diffused throughout the entire being, radiating from the solar man, and permeating the mind and thus entering into the mortal body which is only a covering of the mind physical copulation becomes a well-trained servant of the will, and is found to be a natural, but yet secondary complement. Sex is not confined to the specialized sex-organs. It permeates the entire being. The person who has no conception of his reality other than as a physical entity has not so much as touched the area of spiritual ecstacy which has been alluded to as "the nectar of the gods;" and so infinitely fine and perfect is the plan of Creation that he can not do so until he is fit; and never can he be fit as long as he remains upon the sense-conscious plane and seeks by sexual perversity and debauchery and sexual insanities to touch that exquisite perfection of joy which he intuitively knows evades him.

Thus the sensual man is caught is a beneficent trap; a wise and just and merciful Power has so placed the "Holy of Holies," that it cannot be defiled; it cannot be reached; it cannot be desecrated. It is forever removed from the touch of the unworthy. No man can hope to express the creative power, the sexual realization of a god, through the functions which are not higher in consciousness than those of the animal.

Would you attain to the status of the divine man? If so, do not imagine for a moment that the divine man is less vital than your puny physical powers would suggest. Neither should you imagine that the sex-function, even in its lowest state (lowest because most lacking in love-consciousness), is anything but pure and clean and right and normal in itself; the attitude of the average man and woman invests it with all its uncleanness.

But with all the vile thought which the undeveloped mind has indulged in respecting the sex-relation; with all the man-made laws arrayed against it as though it were criminal, and the teachings of the Church denying its spiritual origin and perpetuation; with women selling it in the public markets for their physical maintenance, nothing less than the fact of the eternality and universality of Sex, as the divine fulcrum of manifestation, can account for the fact that the poor little bi-une Love-god is after all coming to be recognized as the hope and savior of Mankind.

If you would have eternal youth and eternal life and love and wisdom, accept this truth, because nothing else can, or will, save you from the "slings and arrows of outrageous fortune."

Another vague query presents itself to the would-be initiate, and we would like to leave this chapter with no misunderstandings; no misconceptions; no misleading statements, because that which we are here stating is not theory. It is the one eternal, undying, simple and unescapable truth which has withstood the onslaughts of time and ignorance.

The query comes and although it has been answered in previous chapters we will again state it, so that there may be no mistake: If the balance is found in counterpartal sex-union—the one man and the one woman uniting on the solar plane—would not this balance be maintained if only one of the two reached the higher planes of consciousness; in other words, would not the balance be struck by extreme purity on the one hand and extreme impurity on the other?

Again we are reminded that the law of the cosmos is wise; that there are no mistakes nor flaws in the cosmic scheme. The answer is that the union is one of complementaries, and not of antitheses. Each one must be balanced, the nature rounded, the soul awake before union is possible. Thus we are saved from ourselves. We cannot, if we would, really gain at the expense of another, although in temporary things we may appear to do so, because the rich grow richer at the expense of the poor; the tyrant ruler maintains his power at the expense of serfs; but doubt not that *eternal equation* is perfect.

There is still another query: If true sex-union is of the soul, what is to prevent soul-mates from finding each other at the moment of death, regardless of their fitness for godhood, and thus circumventing, as it were, the plan of Creation, which would compel each one to earn the prize of eternal life?

124

The same law governs the interior planes as the exterior. The realization of consciousness is not a capricious matter any more than is the law of physical growth. A man might be in the presence of untold wealth, but if he had not the consciousness to know and realize values, he would remain poor, even though by a wave of his hand he might command millions. One might give a blind man a check for a million dollars, and if he had no others means of knowing what it was, he might easily imagine it to be worthless. Death does not bestow wisdom. Wisdom is acquired. Love is a self-generator.

If you would follow the law of transmutation and acquire the throne of angelhood, get busy within the laboratory of your own mind. Take the crucible of Thought and begin to work interiorly upon the common, everyday things that present themselves in your environment. This is the only way of transmutation. Love grows by feeding upon itself, and the sacrifices and the kindnesses that are bestowed in love without thought of personal benefit grow into the flood of golden light and love of the spiritual realms.

The chief virtue in any one's pursuit of philosophy, or of esoteric wisdom, and in methods of attainment, is found in the fact that such effort is proof of earnest desire to attain. Emerson says that the principal benefit of a college education is to teach the student that he does not need a college education. This estimate of the value of years of study seems at first glance a sarcastic one, but it is not. If this wisdom can be acquired in no other way, then even so it were well worth the price. If the student can learn that much love is the price of transmutation only after exhausting every other method, what does it matter, so that he finally learns it?

Learn to look into the hearts of men.

At first sight, everything on the busy city street is a part of a moving panorama; but an intimate view, when you get in touch with segregated parts of the panorama, discloses the interior nature; the hopes and the fears; the aspirations and the longings and the heartaches and the joys of the entities composing the whole moving picture.

You notice a little female figure; her cheeks are pinked to a hue rivalling the American beauty rose; her lips are carmined like a clowns and her eyebrows penciled too obviously. Her cheap little dress is amateurishly cut in imitation of "the latest." Your first impulse, perhaps, is to scorn her as a "brazen" creature of the streets; but if you will suspend judgment and look a little closer, you may see that her eyes are, in their depths, those of a child, for all her seeming experience. Her brazenness is perhaps only the armor which she has donned to hide a turbulent heart—the dowry of centuries of grandmothers who longed for one glimpse of freedom; of the right to comb their hair as they liked; to powder their faces if they wanted to; to run and jump and laugh and

innocently free and happy without the fear of shocking that
Respectability, and the tyrant Decorum, which insisted that a
man's legs must be carefully concealed on penalty of being adjudged
"immodest."

Those poor reviled, execrated and vigilantly-concealed legs of our fore-mothers! They are crying aloud for vindication, and they will be heard wherever the line of least resistance affords a channel for their freedom. And so, instead of blaming the poor little painted doll of a woman, look into her heart. You will discover that she is bent on having two things long denied womankind—freedom and happiness. If she is foredoomed to failure on the route she has chosen, that is all the more reason why you should withhold censure and give freely of your help and sympathy.

"Learn to look into the hearts of men."

Learn to see beneath the appearance. The old Italian organ-grinder doing his best to please you with his wheezy hurdy-gurdy is not just an old organ-grinder. He is also a man with emotions and feelings and longings and hopes identical in substance with your own; no matter if the organ is out of tune. Learn to hear the *spirit* of the aria or the intermezzo.

And behold! There is a bunch of noisy, dirty, slangy and bold street-arabs—at least that is what they look like from the outside. But learn to look within. There you will find the cause of their appearance, and when you have found the cause you will sympathize with them. If you can get back to the underlying cause of the manifestations of life, you will never fail to sympathize with the condition you may find, even though you find the cause rooted in crime.

You do not have to agree with the criminal in order to sympathize with his misery. If you have the inner vision, which you must have if you would transmute the baser metals into pure gold and find the key to immortal life and love, you will never fail to understand and to sympathize with every point of view. "Whoever walks a furlong without sympathy walks to his own funeral."

Don't imagine for one moment that you have to go to the Himalayas to find the inner vision; or that you will obtain the key to the Hidden Mysteries by shutting yourself in a monastery. Wherever you are, you must lose sight of yourself. Not the higher Self of Reality, but the lesser self of the carnal, or sense-conscious plane—the personality that conceals *you*. And above all, you are not to regard this personality as an enemy to be scourged and beaten and reviled. It is, or it should be, a willing, and helpful servant of your soul even as we say "the hand is the servant of the brain." If your hand becomes unruly and does not obey your brain, train it to do so, don't cut it off, even though the

Bible does appear to tell you to—why should the men who wrote in that far-off time know more of Truth than we of a later century?

You may imagine that you need to belong to some "Brotherhood," in order to learn the secrets of alchemical transmutation. There is nothing of the Great Wisdom which can be taught you, which you cannot learn of yourself if you will look within and unite with the heart of the world.

There is no wisdom higher than love; and there is no power greater than love; and there is no heaven happier than love and there is no God holier than love. If you will take this for your creed you will readily see that it is for you to think love into those things that appear to lack it; think purity into those things that appear impure; think unity into those things that appear separated; and taking the lesson home to your own intimate conduct of life, invest the expression of your sex with the pure and lofty and holy power God gave to it, or refrain from the thought of sex until you can learn to do so.

Says a modern writer: "If you are still so out of tune with the Infinite as to harbor any thought of evil or shame in connection with the specialized organs and functions of sex, let this illumination from on high cast that devil out of your cosmos forever. And if you turn away with soul offended from even 'the slimy gendering of the toad,' you dishonor God who once knew no higher creative formula and still blesses it with His fruitful presence."

And finally do not make the too common mistake of confounding brazenness with freedom from shame and self-condemnation.

Whatever of beauty and purity and joy has come to you in this life has come because of the divinity of Sex. If you have been wise enough to know this, and have reverenced it and purified your mind in respect to that function of your being, you will not cheapen it by parading the subject before those who have no idealism, any more than you would "cast pearls before swine;" you will not countenance jokes and ribald songs; you will not indulge in promiscuousness; but instead you will fold it within the sacred intimacy of your heart's divine altar, as something too beautiful, too holy for the garish light of the un-tender day.

If you have taken into your consciousness the divinity of Sex, you will desire unity and disdain possession, knowing that whatever of Heaven is vouchsafed Mankind here is but a shadow of the reality of spiritual realization of the function of Sex. You will respect the physical body as the handiwork of the Creative Principle of the universe, respecting the sacredness of human life and liberty. You will teach the truth that the law of Life is mathematically just; that nothing will unlock the gates of Eternal Life and Love, except inward honesty; fidelity; unselfishness; spiritual desire.

... these qualities, we are fit for the kingdom of Love and we shall ...ter therein.

...erily Love transforms mere men into immortal gods.

FINIS

CPSIA information can be obtained
at www.ICGtesting.com
Printed in the USA
LVHW041300280820
664156LV00006B/1028